Hu$tle With Fine$$e

Presents

Tri State Triangle
Part 2

Written By

Tamika D. Harding

This is a work of fiction. The author has invented the characters. Any resemblance to actual persons, living or dead is purely coincidental.

If you have purchased this book with a 'dull' or missing cover — you may have possibly purchased an unauthorized or stolen book. Please immediately contact the publisher.

Library of Congress Control Number: 2010901565

ISBN: 978-0-615-35238-1

Cover Design/ Graphics: Jamar Hargrove of Diverse Graphics

Text layout: Tamika D. Harding

Author: Tamika D. Harding

Editor-in-Chief: Tamika D. Harding

Printed in the United States of America

Dedication

I am dedicating this book to all of my fallen soldiers. Whether it's the Music Industry, Book Industry, Comedian, or Actor may you Rest in Peace. Your work made an impact on a lot of people's lives around the world. If it wasn't for you a lot of the people after you wouldn't be where they are. Thanks.

For all of the people whose lives were lost because of this epidemic that they call a game (Drug Game). May you Rest in Peace also. My heart goes out to all of the families that lost their loved ones due to the streets. Keep your heads up they are still alive in your hearts.

Acknowledgements

First of all I would like to thank the almighty GOD for giving me the gift of creativity. Also for giving me the drive to go out and make my goals and dreams come true. I thank him for giving me the strength to get through the rough times. Without him I wouldn't be able to share this gift with all of you that I have recently gained as fans of my work.

Now I would like to thank everyone who purchased my first book "Tri State Triangle" and also this book "Tri State Triangle part 2". I wouldn't be successful without an audience. Thanks for the love and support.

I would like to thank Jamar Hargrove for the excellent work he does with my graphic designs. If it weren't for you I wouldn't have been able to step up my game on the cover designs.

I would like to thank RJ Communications for charging me so much money to do work for me, because without you I wouldn't have been able to learn from my mistakes.

I went from just winging it in this business to being very knowledgeable about the business enough to give advice to others just starting out like myself. I want to thank everyone that helped me learn these lessons.

I would like to thank the Bar Owners in Chester that supported me by letting me sell my books in their establishments and hang up and pass out flyers. I appreciate it.

Table of Contents

Chapter One

Star Status

It was a hot sunny day when Hutch pulled up on the strip in Riverside. He was showing off the brand new BMW 745 series he had just brought the week before. Hutch didn't drive it since the day he bought it home from the dealer. He wanted 22 inch rims on it before he actually drove it.

Hutch was knee deep in the game and it was no turning back now. He was up to a hundred and fifty pounds of weed and a half a brick of cocaine. He was going full throttle at his drug dealings. When Tamia told him to only give her half the money for the last fifty pounds of weed he would ever buy from her. He took that extra money and expanded his business by buying nine ounces of cocaine. He turned that into eighteen ounces almost overnight. He never realized how much money there was to be made from cocaine in Wilmington until he brought those nine ounces.

There was no sign of Juice anywhere. But Hutch still never left home without his bulletproof vest. With Juice still on his mind he paid for extra muscle out on the strip in Riverside.

"What's up Hutch? I see you with the big boy beamer, 22's huh? You're stunting hard too." Troy spoke as Hutch got out of the car.

"Yeah you know I had to treat myself playboy, you'll have one of these one day if you keep hustling hard like this." Hutch responded as he collected his money from Troy.

"Oh most definitely, you know I'm stacking T-Roy not out here for nothing." Troy responded talking in a third person.

"That's what I like to hear, smart hustlers have longevity. Come pass the spot to pick up your re up in like an hour." Hutch said as he got back in the car to pull away.

"I almost got this city sowed up I feel like the Mayor of Wilmington." Hutch thought to himself as he drove away. Finally he was feeling alive again after the deaths of his cousin and side kick.

After he found another weed connect and a new connect on the best cocaine in the Tri State area. Hutch was the man to see whether you were a Fiend, Pothead or buying weight. He had at least thirty people on his payroll.

Hutch wanted to make sure everybody around him was making money. When you want to be a leader in order for you to have followers you must ask yourself this question. Is it better to be feared or loved? Hutch asked himself that very question. The answer he came up with was loved and respected. That way no one would slit his throat because he's putting money in their pockets. They respect him because they know he's not going to let anyway stand in his way from making it to the top.

When Hutch got to his stash house he counted the money Troy had given him. He then made up his next bundle for Troy to pick up in an hour. Troy was 17 and about to graduate from high school. He was one of Hutch's protégés. All the teenagers looked up to Hutch and Hutch had love for all of them.

An hour had passed when Troy knocked on the door.

"What's up Old Head, you ready for me? I'm sold out, here's the rest of your money." Troy said as he handed Hutch fifteen hundred dollars.

"Yeah here keep a stack and give me the rest youngen. Do you have all of your prom gear together or you still shopping?" Hutch asked thinking of letting him drive the BMW to the prom.

"Yeah I'm done, I got a black suit with Gucci on the cuffs and the collar and some Gucci shoes to match. You know I got to stunt at my Prom." Troy responded.

"Yeah you better you representing me. You can't call me old head and go out half ass." Hutch responded as he walked out with him.

"I get money, money I got, I get." 50 cent came through the speakers as Hutch's phone rang.

"What's up fam?" Hutch answered. "Yo Hutch I need to get at you in like a half I'm out." Rahmir said on the other end.

"Alright man, meet me at the spot I'll be there in like fifteen minutes." Hutch responded as he walked to his car.

He made his way over to the other side of Wilmington to his other stash house to meet Rahmir. He didn't stand on the strip or the corner any more. He had too many workers and too many wholesale customers for that.

When Hutch pulled up Rahmir was already there waiting. Rahmir had just sold his last twenty bag of cocaine when he called Hutch. So he was eager to get more from him so he could go back to the block to get more money.

"Damn Rah you're moving this shit real quick." Hutch spoke as he shook his hand.

"Yeah well you know I never been in the way out here Old Head I hold it down." Rahmir responded really wanting to skip the small talk.

"I see that, you want one or two ounces this time." Hutch asked.

"I want two I told you I hold it down out here." Rahmir responded a little agitated.

"Alright soldier, come on in so I can get that to you." Hutch responded as he headed inside the house.

"Out of all the days to procrastinate he picked the day the block is popping and I'm out of dope." Rahmir thought to himself.

"Alright cannon here, give me back two stacks off of that when you're done." Hutch responded as he walked Rahmir out.

"Alright old head I'll hit you as soon as I'm done." Rahmir said as he rushed to go somewhere to bag up the two ounces Hutch had just given him.

Rahmir had turned twenty one the week before. He had everything going for him but just couldn't leave the streets alone. He played football for Delaware University. He majored in Business management. Rahmir had one year of college left before he graduated. NFL scouts were looking at Rahmir. That fast money took a tight hold of him and he didn't want it to let go.

In an hour Rahmir was back on the block conducting business as usual. He had a small beef with some of the boys who sold drugs a couple blocks down from where he did. So he wasn't taking any chances of them trying to steal his clientele.

After Hutch finished making his rounds he went home to see his girlfriend Sherelle and their son Derron Jr.

Sherelle got used to living in Chester after she had the baby. During the day she attended Delaware County Community College. Hutch didn't want her to work so she became a full time mother and student.

"Relle , Where you at?" Hutch yelled as he entered their apartment.

"I'm in lil Derron's room trying to put him to sleep now here you come all loud." Sherelle responded.

"Oops I'm sorry, well since he's up look what daddy got his little man." Hutch said as he handed his son a football.

"You are going to spoil him, doesn't he have enough stuff?" Sherelle responded.

"Nope my little man is going to have everything he wants." Hutch responded.

"Yeah well make sure you stay alive to watch him grow up, when are you going to stop hustling anyway?" Sherelle asked.

"I will as soon as I get financially comfortable." Hutch responded taking the now awaken Derron Jr. away from Sherelle.

"Well when are you going to be comfortable?" Sherelle asked as she watched Hutch put Derron Jr. in bed for his nap.

"Well after you graduate and I reach a certain amount of money." Hutch responded not really wanting to have this conversation.

"Well if you say so I just hope everything ends how you plan it." Sherelle responded as she headed for the bathroom to take a shower.

"I'm glad she didn't keep talking about it I don't feel like arguing right now." Hutch thought to himself as he headed for the kitchen to get something to eat.

"I'm a hustler, I'm a, I'm a hustler homey." Cassidy came through the speakers of Hutch's phone.

"What's up my dude?" Hutch answered.

“You’re never going to guess what just went down my dude.” Styles said on the other end of the phone.

“What?” Hutch asked.

“That dude Juice you’re beefing with came on the block asking for you. He said he’s trying to squash the beef. He want to buy some weed from you because his connect got out the game and he can’t find nobody else to cop from. He also said he pump down B more.” Styles said in an as a matter of fact tone.

“What? Yo dude got some fucking nerve either that nigga Bold as shit or stupid as hell.” Hutch responded.

“Yo, what do you want me to do? Because he said he’ll be back with some paper if you want to squash it and do business.” Styles asked.

"Meet me at the spot in the A.M, I'd rather think about it and tell you face to face." Hutch replied.

Hutch was smiling from ear to ear after he hung up the phone. He hadn't gotten news like this in a while. This was a big opportunity that Hutch was waiting on for a long time now. He couldn't believe that Juice was giving himself to him on a silver platter. Now exactly how he was going to execute this is what he had to contemplate.

After satisfying his hunger with some leftovers he had heated up, Hutch waited for Sherelle to finish with her shower. He wanted to celebrate with some good sex. Sherelle was in for the night of her life. All Hutch had to worry about was their son waking up during their escapade.

As soon as Sherelle entered the room, Hutch came from behind the door and grabbed her from behind. He slowly caressed her thick thighs as he worked his way up to her breast. Squeezing and gently stroking her nipples as he lightly licked her neck.

Sherelle became instantly aroused. Before Hutch could finish his foreplay she started some of her own. Sherelle eased out of his clutches to turn around so she could kiss him as passionately as he was caressing her. As she stuck her tongue inside of his mouth she let her hands wander down his six pack to his manhood and vigorously stroked it until it became too hard for her to stroke while still inside of his pants. She eased his pants and boxers down at the same time. That put her in the position they both wanted. She placed his manhood into her mouth and began to suck and stroke so good hutch could barely continue to stand up.

Hutch couldn't take it anymore. He pulled away then picked Sherelle up and spun her up against the wall all in one motion. She became even more aroused by his aggressive behavior. The front of her was up against the wall as he peeled her waist off of it just enough for him to slide himself right inside. He had both her arms pinned up against the wall with one hand and her leg in the other hand as Hutch stroked away at her soak and wet vagina. His stroke got deeper with every moan she made.

Finally he pulled his manhood out of her then picked her up and carried her over to the bed. Once there he laid her down. He put himself back inside of her while he was still standing. Again stroking away at her soak and wet vagina until the both of them had an orgasm.

"Boy this is why I will never leave you." Sherelle said as her body trembled then collapsed.

"Oh so you're only with a brother cause his stroke game is tight huh?" Hutch said jokingly as he headed to the kitchen for something to drink.

Sherelle took that opportunity to pull her exhausted body up to the head of the bed. She was fast asleep before Hutch came back inside of the bedroom.

"Damn, and I was coming back for round two. Oh well I do need to get some sleep too." Hutch thought to himself as he climbed in the bed with her.

He kissed her on her cheek and said good night before he closed his eyes to fall asleep.

Chapter Two

Vengeance gone bad

"Who the hell could this be knocking at the door this time of night?" Sanaa questioned to herself. When she looked out through the peep hole, she didn't see any one. She waited to see if they would show their face a few minutes later. Still there was no one in sight. Again there was a knock at the door but this time Sanaa went for her gun.

Tamia was still sitting on the couch in a daze. Sanaa headed back towards the door. There was another knock at the door before she made it there. Again there was no one in sight when she looked through the peep hole.

"Oh y'all want to play games, huh." Sanaa thought to herself. She took the chain off the door, cocked her pistol, and unlocked the door. She took a deep breath as she began to turn the knob to proceed with opening the door.

Sanaa was alert and ready to shoot when she opened the door to a crack. Bourbon's brother Shawn kicked the door in and shot Tamia in the arm as she tried to run. Sanaa was thrown back a bit when the door swung open but still kept her balance. She was behind him when he shot Tamia and returned a few shots of her own.

One of the bullets pierced Shawn's shoulder as he turned to shoot at Sanaa. The shot he got off hit Sanaa in the stomach. She stumbled as she fell back towards the bathroom. After a few steps she hit the wall and slowly slid down it with her gun still inside of her hand. She refused to let that gun go no matter what.

Stunned by the bullet Shawn couldn't raise his arm to return another shot. Tamia took that opportunity to grab the gun she had hidden under the couch to return some shots of her own. One of Tamia's bullets hit Shawn in his chest. He then immediately fell to the floor. The neighbor across the hall came rushing in after he got his gun to see if the girls needed help. When he entered the apartment he kicked the gun away from Shawn's hand. Afterwards he called the cops and told them he needed an officer and a paramedic.

"Are you okay Tamia? Do you know this guy?" the neighbor asked.

"Yeah I used to hang around with his sister. He was the one who broke into Sanaa's apartment in Delaware and our shop. We got him locked up so he's probably here for revenge." Tamia replied.

"Wow, Sanaa are you still with us? An ambulance is on the way so hold on." The neighbor turned his attention towards Sanaa.

"I got you baby here's a towel just put pressure on it." Tamia said also turning her attention towards Sanaa.

"We got to get out of her Mia." Sanaa whispered to Tamia.

"We will but we got to get you to the emergency room first you bleeding everywhere." Tamia responded.

The neighbor just sat on the couch with his gun pointed at Shawn so he wouldn't try to make any sudden moves before the police showed up. He always protected Tamia since the day she moved in. Sanaa was no exception a friend of Tamia's was a friend of his also.

All Sanaa could think about was going to jail. She had just killed Ice about an hour ago and now shot Shawn with the same gun. But had she got rid of the gun before they got home, she and Tamia would both be dead.

“Mia come here I have to tell you something.” Sanaa said feeling weaker by the minute.

“What is it Sanaa?” Tamia responded hoping she wasn’t going to say she wasn’t going to make it.

“Can you come a little closer? I have to tell you in your ear.” Sanaa responded only wanting Tamia to hear her.

Tamia leaned in. “What is it Sanaa?” Tamia asked.

“This is the same gun I used to kill Ice with. I’m going to jail if the cops get here and investigate.” Sanaa replied.

“So how do you suggest we get out of this one? They should be pulling up any minute now.” Tamia responded.

“I don’t know but we need to get out of here, and get him out of here so he doesn’t get suspicious.” Sanaa responded as they heard the Sirens getting closer.

“It’s too late now S they’re coming.” Tamia whispered.

Tamia got up off of the floor to wrap her arm up. She wanted to try to stop some of her own bleeding.

“Is that pussy still breathing?” Tamia said as she walked by Shawn to get a towel.

Sanaa took that opportunity to push her gun inside the vent in the bathroom while no one was looking. She knew the vent was already loose. Sanaa had called about a week ago for someone to come out and tighten it up. At this moment she was glad that no one ever came.

"Yeah he's still breathing I'm making sure of that." The neighbor responded.

In a matter of minutes the police were at the door asking questions. Ten minutes later the paramedics were walking through the door. After the police got statements from the neighbor and Tamia they didn't need a statement from Shawn. His motive was clear to the police. Tamia had a registered gun and license to carry. The police didn't question that weapon because they saw the paper work. The other gun that was visible to them was Shawn's. He was facing charges of Gun possession, assault with a deadly weapon, reckless endangerment, home invasion, attempted murder, and last but not least violation of parole. He was going away for a long time.

The paramedic took Sanaa and Shawn to the ambulance first. Then Tamia squeezed in after she gave her statement. The officers called headquarters to arrange for twenty four hour security for Shawn so he wouldn't escape.

The neighbor followed the ambulance to the hospital to make sure Tamia and Sanaa were fine. They kept Sanaa so he left when Tamia was released. The bullet went through Tamia's arm. She was treated and released in a matter of hours.

The next morning Tamia tried hard to gather her thoughts. She had one hell of a night and needed to go somewhere to relax. But under the circumstances she couldn't go anywhere. Sanaa was in the hospital. The shop needed her attention more than ever now. She needed to take care of her clients and Sanaa's.

Before she went to the shop she went to the hospital to check on Sanaa. The doctors had performed emergency surgery to take the bullet out of her stomach before it traveled through her body. Sanaa was exhausted and still drugged but happy to see Tamia when she walked through the door.

"Hey Mia, I thought you weren't coming are you still mad at me?" Sanaa asked barely able to speak.

"Hey, don't try to talk you need your rest. I was just coming to check on you before I went to the shop. You're going to be in here for at least two to three weeks. I'm going to have to take your clients. My arm is sore I don't know how I'm going to get through this week but I have to handle business." Tamia replied.

"I'm sorry Mia I don't know what came over me." Sanaa mumbled.

"Don't try to talk right now gain your strength back first. We'll talk later about all of this. Get well first and I'm not mad I'm just a little mind boggled over this whole thing but you handled yourself like a soldier when Shawn came through the door shooting. I didn't know you had in you like that." Tamia responded.

"Thank you Mia." Sanaa responded trying to sit up.

"No you rest I'll be back tonight or tomorrow morning. It depends on what kind of day I have at the shop today. Oh and I got what you put inside of the vent in the bathroom and threw it away." Tamia responded.

"Thank you I don't know what I'd do without you Mia." Sanaa whispered.

"Alright S I'm out I have to get to the shop Amber and Keisha are probably swamped." Tamia said before she turned to leave.

She kissed Sanaa on her forehead before she left.

It took Tamia ten minutes to get to the shop. She needed to gather her thoughts before she walked inside.

Doing hair was the last thing Tamia wanted to do. She knew the girls would ask questions when they saw the bandage. She needed to prepare herself for what she had in store for her.

"Hi." Tamia spoke as she entered the shop.

"Hey Tamia, What happened to you?" Amber asked.

"I got shot and I don't feel like Talking about it right now." Tamia responded.

"Oh okay well are you okay?" Amber asked being concerned.

"I'll be alright once I can take a vacation." Tamia responded.

"I know that's right. Hey wait a minute where is Sanaa."Keisha asked joining the conversation.

"She's in the hospital she was shot in her stomach." Tamia responded.

"Well is she okay? Damn y'all had a rough night." Keisha asked.

"She will be. Come on Ms. Ruth I have to take you today Sanaa's in the hospital." Tamia responded.

"Well okay I hope she gets better." Ms. Ruth replied.

"I hope so too Ms.Ruth." Tamia responded as she took her over to the sink to wash her hair.

The rest of her and Sanaa's appointments started to walk in. Tamia handled the situation. But was tired of explaining where Sanaa was. After a long day Tamia was exhausted and needed a drink. She went to Club Tonyx to unwind. That wasn't her usual spot but she wanted to see what the hype was about.

"This is a nice spot I like the inside. Sanaa would love this." Tamia thought to herself as she walked toward the bar.

"Can I have a bottle of Moet please?" Tamia asked the bar maid.

"Sure White Star, Nectar, or Rose'?" She asked.

"I'll take the Nectar please thank you." Tamia responded.

After Tamia paid for her bottle she took a seat at one of the tables by the catwalk. There were three poles for the girls to dance. Tamia attended a few strip clubs but never one that had three girls dancing at the same time. For the first time in a long time Tamia was actually enjoying herself.

One stripper in particular couldn't take her eyes off of Tamia. She thought Tamia was so gorgeous. She continued to give her performance. But as soon as she was done she wasted no time making her way over to where Tamia was sitting.

"Hi sexy I'm Cocoa. What's your name Mami?" The stripper asked.

"I'm Tamia nice to meet you." Tamia responded.

"So what brings you to Tonyx?" Cocoa asked.

"I needed to unwind so I figured I'd come here and get a show while I was at it." Tamia responded.

"Well sexy did I do a good job at entertaining you?" Cocoa asked.

"Yeah I guess so I was watching all three of you. All of you were fine." Tamia responded.

“So do you like lap dances or do you just like to watch the dancers on the pole.” Cocoa asked.

“I just like to watch honey lap dances don’t do anything for me.” Tamia responded focusing her attention back to the dancers on the pole.

“So do you date strippers?” Cocoa asked.

“I never have I actually only been with one female.” Tamia responded.

“So can I see you outside of this club? I’m not your average stripper I just dance I don’t have sex for money. I’m in school during the day. I’m a business major.” Cocoa asked hoping Tamia would say yes.

“Actually mami I do have a girlfriend. We live together and we are partners. We own a hair salon together.” Tamia responded.

"Well that's too bad you are so sexy too." Cocoa responded.

"Yeah well maybe if I become free one day." Tamia answered.

"Well, take my number just in case that does happen. How can you give me a chance if you don't have the number? I'm almost done with school so I will not be working here too much longer. You need to know how to get in touch with me." Cocoa responded being persistent.

"Listen I'll take your number down, but if my girlfriend goes through my phone and calls you she's very jealous and crazy as hell. So tell her you are a new client you were looking for a new stylist but I haven't called you yet." Tamia responded.

"Well it will not be a lie where is your shop I do need a new stylist?" Cocoa responded.

"It's in Chester but please don't start anything with her. I'll give you a chance if I become single." Tamia responded.

Cocoa got exactly what she wanted. They exchanged numbers. Tamia enjoyed the rest of her night while Cocoa went back to work. She had spent her entire break talking to Tamia. After another hour had passed Tamia made her exit out of the club to go home.

Chapter Three

Good News

Gunz and Hammer flew to Florida to find Fonnie. It took a month of being in the Orange State to find him urinating behind a local bodega in Miami. They decided to take him back to Philadelphia to get more compensation for him.

“I know you didn’t think you were really going to get away now did you?” Gunz asked with his .357 caliber pistol pointed at Fonnie’s head.

“I just left the state I got out of the way man. Spazz said I was finished in Philly. So I’m down here trying to start over.” Fonnie said trying to fast talk them into not killing him.

"Well as a matter of fact Spazz and Hector would like to see you. They want to have a word with you. So we're taking you back to Philly." Hammer added to the conversation.

"But I got shit popping down here a little bit man. Why y'all taking a nigga back up north?" Fonnie responded running out of things to say to get out of the situation.

"Like he' said nigga, Spazz and Hector would like to see you. It seems that you three have some unfinished business to discuss." Gunz replied as he smacked him in the back of the head with the .357.

While Fonnie was out cold Gunz and Hammer both put him in the trunk of his own car then drove him back to Philly. It took them three days to finally get back to South Philadelphia. As soon as they touched down they took him to Tamia's old stash house. Gunz had his .357 pointed at the trunk while Hammer slowly opened it. Fonnie tried to fight his way out of there to no avail. Gunz smacked him in the head again with the gun knocking him out cold yet again. They drug him inside and tied him up. Hammer immediately called Carlos.

"Good News playboy, Gunz and I have a present for you. Make sure you bring them birds with you. We're at the spot." Hammer said before he hung up

"I can't wait until he gets here with them birds. We are going straight to go bag that work up boy. You are about to make us two rich men. Fucking conniving ass nigga." Gunz said to Fonnie with a smirk.

"Shouldn't we call Spazz too?" Hammer asked.

"Oh yeah I almost forgot."Gunz responded as he started to dial Tamia's number.

"Yizzo." Tamia answered.

"What's up Spazz? Long time no hear. Look we at the spot and we got a present for you. Someone decided to come back from Florida." Gunz said anxious to get his hands on those kilos.

"Alright good work I'll be there shortly." Tamia said as she started to head out the door.

"Damn I'm really not up for this but this shit has to be over with and fast so I can move on." Tamia thought to herself as she pulled off.

Thirty minutes later Tamia showed up. Carlos showed up five minutes later. Tamia handed Gunz the duffle bag full of cocaine for bringing Fonnie back alive.

“Oh now we can get this party started.” Gunz said when he saw Tamia holding the duffle bag with the cocaine in it.

“Yeah now it’s on, our job here is done nice to know you Fonnie.” Hammer added to the conversation.

Fonnie reacted the same way Flex did when he saw Carlos. Spazz wasted no time getting to the point. She didn’t want to be there in the first place.

“Take the tape off of his mouth Hammer.” Tamia ordered.

“No Problem.” Hammer responded.

“So you thought you had this all figured out huh? What, you forgot I was a boss? No one crosses me and gets away with it Fonnie. What was that shit you were talking that I’m not built and something like I can’t put an end to your career out here on these streets?” Tamia started the conversation.

"No Spazz let me explain it was all flex idea I just went along with it because me and him go back to childhood. I told him it wasn't a good idea." Fonnie tried to plead his case to no avail.

"Tape his mouth back." Carlos ordered. "I'm tired of hearing him acting like a bitch man up for once. Own up to your shit you fucked up. Now it's time to face the consequences." Carlos interrupted irritated by Fonnie.

Gunz happily taped his mouth back shut as he taunted Fonnie.

"I always knew you pissed sitting down your skirt been up to me a long time ago." Gunz said to Fonnie with a smirk on his face.

Carlos put his gun to Fonnie's head and squeezed the trigger. Tamia handed Gunz the duffle bag before she headed for the door.

"Clean this mess up and make sure you call me or Hector for your re up when y'all are finished with those bricks." Carlos said before he made his exit.

After Hammer and Gunz cleaned up and dumped the body. They went to the block. The same blocks Tamia ran and Flex and Fonnie took over and expanded. They hustled harder than they ever had in their lives. After a month they were ready to re up with Hector and Carlos. They had their minds made up that they would be the new Kings of Philly. It was to the top or broke for them and broke wasn't an option.

Gunz phoned Hector before they completely ran out of their supply. Hammer couldn't wait until they got their re up.

Hector's phone rang while he was in his office at his club in Camden.

"Hello." Hector answered.

"What's up Hec? I need to see you my man asap." Gunz said on the other end.

"Ok I'm at the club right now come through so we can talk." Hector replied before he hung up the phone.

"It's our time Hammer! It's official after this flip we are going to be the new Kings of Philly." Gunz said excitedly.

"Yeah man I can't wait how long did he say?" Hammer anxiously inquired.

"He said come now." Gunz responded.

"Alright well let's go get these birds." Hammer responded with a sense of urgency.

Growing up Hammer and Gunz were very close. Gunz was nine years old when he and his family moved on the same block as Hammer and his family. They used to do everything together.

While playing baseball and football in the middle of the street. Hammer and Gunz both admired the local drug dealers. They all had on two finger rings, thick rope chains, kept their hair freshly cut, and what they admired the most? They all had nice cars and women falling to their feet.

At the age of fourteen they both had their minds made up that this is what they wanted for themselves when they grew up.

There was one thing they didn't know about the life a drug dealer leads. And that was many lives are destroyed because of it. Families lose their loved ones to the product and other families lose their loved ones to the prison system. Some dealers make it harder on themselves to live normal lives. They can't get jobs because of their police records. Last but not least some fall to a bullet.

"Come on in guys have a seat how's the game been treating you?" Hector asked before they could knock on the door, it was already ajar.

"It's been good that's why we're here." Hammer answered as he and Gunz walked through the half opened door.

"I see, so have you guys been taking precautions? The game is changing as we speak." Hector responded.

"Yeah we are you can't be too careful." Hammer responded.

"We are trying to get rich not jail sentences besides we came up under Spazz shouldn't that speak for itself?" Gunz added hating when Hector underestimated him.

"Well then let's take care of business I don't want to hold you two up any longer." Hector responded.

"That's what I'm talking about we want ten birds." Gunz responded as he handed Hector the money.

“Well okay then wait here I’ll be back in ten minutes.” Hector responded.

“Yo I can’t wait to go bag up this work.” Hammer said excitedly as he rubbed his hands together.

“Yeah me either but first I need to go see my girl I’m a little backed up.” Gunz responded as he thought of how long it’s been since he had sex.

“Yeah I need to do the same. Now that you mentioned it I haven’t burst one in a minute. We were too busy on our grind.” Hammer said with a chuckle in his voice.

“We were on our grind heavy I can’t wait to get back to the block.” Gunz responded.

After fifteen minutes Hector came back into the office. He placed a duffle bag with twenty kilos in it on his desk.

“It’s twenty in there I’m going to front you guys ten to keep you out of my hair for a while." Hector said bringing smiles to both of their faces.

"Okay bet you don't know how much you just looked out." Hammer responded as he grabbed the handle to the duffle bag.

"Yeah good looking we needed that right there." Gunz added as he got up to leave.

"You boys be careful out there I'll see you on your next re up." Hector responded as he walked them to the door.

They left Hector's office smiling from ear to ear. They were starting to shine like the sun peeping out from behind the clouds.

They were on their way to being the supplier to the whole city of Philadelphia. Even with all the money they were making, they still remained humbled. They made sure they treated all of their workers fair. They even made sure all of the kids were taken care of in South Philly. None of them was a have not thanks to Hammer and Gunz.

CHAPTER FOUR

Something New

After a long day at the shop Tamia decided to take a hot bubble bath to unwind. She had settled the score with Fonnie the night before. Earlier that day she had a heated discussion with Sanaa.

“Sanaa is really starting to stress me out and I don’t know what to do about it.” Tamia thought to herself as she stepped her thick naked caramel body into the bath tub.

“First she stresses me about leaving the streets alone. Then she kills Ice in a jealous rage. How can my life turn upside down in a matter of months? I just stopped selling drugs and as soon as I do she brings drama deadly drama at that." Tamia continued to think to herself as she relaxed in the steaming hot bubble bath she ran herself.

Tamia was so relaxed by the hot water and aroma therapy candles burning, she had fallen asleep. Tamia was awakened by the water turning cold. After about forty five minutes of relaxation. She decided to bath and get out of the bath tub.

Once she entered the bedroom Tamia looked for the lotion. Once she found it she slowly rubbed it all over her body. She caressed every inch of herself as she moistened her skin. She then slipped on a silk negligee and started flipping through channels on the television.

"I should call Cocoa to see what she's up to. I need someone to talk to. The longer Sanaa stays in the hospital the more she's going to stress me out." Tamia thought to herself.

"I think I will do just that." Tamia continued her thoughts as she reached for her phone to dial Cocoa's number.

"Hello." Cocoa answered in the sexiest voice she could muster up.

"Hello may I speak with Cocoa?" Tamia asked.

"This is she may I ask who I am speaking with?" Cocoa responded.

"This is Tamia the female you met at Tonyx the other night and I told you I had a girlfriend. You insisted that I take your number anyway. Do you remember or do you come on to females on a regular basis?" Tamia responded trying to refresh her memory.

"No, I don't come on to females on a regular basis and yes I know exactly who you are. You are the sexy hairstylist with the girlfriend as a partner from the other night. How could I forget about you? Is it my turn to get my chance?" Cocoa answered in an as a matter of fact tone.

"Well not yet I'm stressed and lonely and needed someone to talk to. You sounded like someone I would like to get to know when we spoke the other night. I was thinking of you so I decided to call." Tamia responded.

"That's a start. It will not be long before you leave her for me." Cocoa said flirting with Tamia.

"Is that right? What makes you so sure?" Tamia responded playfully.

"Because you called when you were feeling lonely and stressed. You are giving me a way in whether you know it or not." Cocoa responded.

“I never thought of it that way. It’s just that my girlfriend is in the hospital. She’s stressing me even from there. She’s too jealous. I don’t want to hurt her or lose our friendship but I’m not sure if I’m even happy anymore.” Tamia said letting out a sigh of relief.

“Well you seem like your mind is already made up on what you want to do. Just woman up and do it.” Cocoa responded not holding any punches.

“I don’t know if it’s already made up or not but I also have too much invested to just up and leave.” Tamia explained.

“Well no one said you had to do it tomorrow. Just slowly do what you have to do. Don’t make it obvious though. If she’s jealous that can be a disaster.” Cocoa responded trying to give good advice.

"It sounds like you know her already, but seriously I can't take it any more Cocoa." Tamia responded.

"Well I guess I was right, you aren't happy with your girlfriend, that's why I gave you my number any way. I knew you would call." Cocoa said in a confident tone.

"Is that right? What made you so sure? If she wasn't stressing me I wouldn't have called." Tamia responded.

"It was the signal you were giving off. I could just tell you were stressed and unhappy." Cocoa responded.

Tamia and Cocoa stayed up on the phone until four o'clock in the morning. They made plans to go out on Sunday. That was the only day Tamia was free. She was busy in the shop since Sanaa was in the hospital for another week.

When Tamia woke up later that morning she was exhausted. She was feeling good about her conversation with Cocoa, so to her it was well worth staying up all night.

Tamia did her usual routine that morning. She got dressed, went to the hospital to see Sanaa, and went to the salon.

As the week went by she became more anxious about her date with Cocoa. She planned a nice day for the both of them. In the afternoon they would catch a Matinee at the movie theater. In the evening they would go to Warm Daddies to enjoy some jazz.

It was Friday morning when Tamia started getting a funny feeling in her stomach. Something wasn't quite right and she couldn't put her finger on it. Tamia always got that gut feeling when something was about to happen. She went about her day in spite of the feeling she was getting. Tamia just prayed that whatever it was wouldn't be fatal.

When Tamia got to the hospital the feeling she had came back. Still she ignored it as she went to Sanaa's room.

"Hey Mia guess what?" Sanaa asked before Tamia got all the way inside the room.

"What is it Sanaa?" Tamia responded dryly.

"Why did you say it like that? And I said guess." Sanaa responded picking up on the fact that Tamia seemed irritated.

"I don't want to guess just tell me I'm tired and not in the mood right now. I had a long day yesterday and another one today when I get to the shop. Now what is it?" Tamia demanded.

"Well I'm going home today I was trying to surprise you but since you're in a bad mood you ruined it." Sanaa responded disappointed.

"I thought you were in here for at least another week?" Tamia responded with a puzzled look on her face.

"No I'm getting discharged today, now as a matter of fact. You sound like you don't want me to come home." Sanaa responded getting offended.

"No it's not that, I just don't have anything planned for you to come home like a welcome home party or something." Tamia responded thinking she might have to cancel her date with Cocoa.

"Well I didn't want a welcome home party anyway I just want to get back to the shop. I know my clients must miss me." Sanaa responded.

"Yes they do, they will be happy to see you. So when are you coming back to the shop?" Tamia asked.

"Today, I knew you'd be here before you went there so that's how I was able to surprise you." Sanaa said with a big smile on her face.

"Well okay, grab your stuff and come on let's go." Tamia responded not really liking the fact that she was being released.

"My stomach is still sore but I think I can still do hair, my stomach will be fine. It's been feeling better since they took out the bullet. I can't believe I actually got shot in my stomach." Sanaa responded.

"Yeah that's why I think you should rest up and not be in such a hurry to get back to work." Tamia responded.

"That's the only way I'm going to fully heal, is if I'm near you. I missed you not being able to lie next to me at night." Sanaa responded.

"Now I have to make an excuse to get out Sunday." Tamia thought to herself.

“Yeah well you don’t have to worry about that now.” Tamia responded.

“I know because I’m out of here now, have you been being good while I was in there?” Sanaa asked.

“Of course I have, but I think you should wait until you heal a little more before you go back to the shop but whatever.” Tamia suggested.

“Yeah I know but I need this I’ve been losing my mind in this hospital room.” Sanaa responded as she checked out of the hospital.

“Alright well we’re on our way there I hope you’re really up for this.” Tamia responded.

“I am but you sound like you don’t want to be bothered with me or something are you mad at me?” Sanaa asked.

“I’m just tired and in need of a vacation that’s all.” Tamia responded as they pulled up to the shop.

“Well when do we leave?” Sanaa responded.

“Maybe I need to go by myself to clear my head.” Tamia answered as she got out of her Escalade.

“Are you mad at me because of Ice? You’re mad about something, so don’t say you’re not.” Sanaa responded as she got out of the Escalade also.

“I just want to get this day over with Sanaa, so please, not right now. I don’t feel like a heated conversation ok.” Tamia responded as she opened the door to the shop.

“Hi Sanaa, How are you feeling girl?” Amber asked before Sanaa had a chance to answer Tamia.

“I’m doing okay my stomach is still a little sore but I’m happy to be back.” Sanaa responded.

“Well welcome back girl we missed you.” Keisha responded.

“I missed y’all too.” Sanaa responded forgetting about the discussion she had just had with Tamia.

“Tamia, why didn’t you tell us Sanaa was coming back today? We don’t have anything planned for her or anything.” Amber snapped at Tamia.

“I just found out today myself. Yell at Sanaa she’s the one who wanted it to be a surprise, I wanted to plan something too.” Tamia snapped back.

“I didn’t want anyone to make a fuss. I just wanted to come back and do hair that’s all. Y’all can respect that right?” Sanaa interrupted coming to her own defense.

"Yeah we can respect that." All three girls said in unison.

As soon as they opened the door to the shop their appointments started walking in. Everyone was so excited to see Sanaa back at work that it became a welcome home party anyway. All the commotion distracted Sanaa from the conversation she had with Tamia before they walked into the shop. That's the way Tamia wanted to keep it as she sat there trying to figure out a way to keep her date on Sunday.

CHAPTER FIVE

Juice Returns

"Say hello to the bad guy, they say I'm a bad guy, I come from the bottom but now I'm mad fly." Jay-Z came through the speakers of Hutch's phone.

"Yo what's up Styles? Come to my spot in like a half." Hutch answered the phone not even waiting for a response to his greeting.

"All right my dude." Styles said on the other end of the phone.

Forty Five minutes later Styles came knocking at Hutch's door. He was in such a hurry to get to the door that he almost tripped over a pair of shoes. After Hutch rapidly opened up the door to let him in they began their discussion.

“So you’re telling me that, this dude wants me to be his connect?” Hutch asked starting the conversation off.

“Yeah my dude, that’s what he said, I don’t know if this is a set up or he’s serious but it seemed like he’s serious to me my dude.” Styles answered.

“So how much is this dude talking? How many pounds he want?” Hutch asked.

“I don’t know he just said he wanted to cop some weed from you. Squash the beef that’s it. That’s all he said.” Styles responded.

“Okay, Look we definitely are going to take that lame dude’s money. Then murder him.” Hutch said with a look of vengeance in his eyes.

“I knew you were thinking about something like that.” Styles responded with a chuckle.

“Alright so set up a meeting with that lame. Let me know what his order is.” Hutch responded.

Styles agreed as he headed for the door with a new swagger. He was happy to know that his Boss wasn’t slipping like he thought. Styles wasted no time following through with Hutch’s orders.

“Say hello to the bad guy they say I’m a bad guy, I came from the bottom but now I’m mad fly.” Jay-z again came through the speakers of Hutch’s phone.

“Yo what’s up?” Hutch responded.

“I’m done Old Head.” Rahmir answered.

“Alright youngen come through.” Hutch answered.

Rahmir got to Hutch in twenty minutes. He was trying to make another two thousand before he called it a night. Rahmir had a big game the following day. There was going to be an NFL scout there to watch him play. There were rumors that The Dallas Cowboys were interested in him.

Rahmir didn't want to believe the rumors until he actually got drafted. So he continued on his path of making fast money.

"What's up Youngen come on in, I see you're grinding hard?" Hutch said when he opened the door.

"Look Old Head, I need four and a half. That'll last me for the rest of the night and when I get home from my game tomorrow. They say a scout from the NFL is going to be there, but I'll wait until tomorrow to see what's what." Rahmir responded.

"Ok youngen that's what it is then. Remember your Old Head when you get to the League." Hutch responded with a chuckle.

"Like I said Old Head I'll believe it when I talk to a scout. I'll get at you when I knock this work off. Are you coming to the game tomorrow?" Rahmir asked.

"You know I'll be there to support you Super Star." Hutch responded.

"Ok, well I'll see you at the game then." Rahmir responded as he walked out the door.

Rahmir was back on the strip in an hour. He had bagged up enough cocaine to reach his goal for the night. When Ramir reached fifteen hundred dollars, the police pulled up on the strip. It was unexpected since the police never patrolled through that project. Everyone that was out on the strip hustling scattered, Rahmir was the one who took off running first, and an officer took off right after him.

“Damn, these bastards never come through here. I can’t let them catch me I got a game tomorrow.” Rahmir thought to himself.

“Freeze.” The Officer shouted.

Rahmir just kept running for dear life. The Officer was starting to lose his breath when Rahmir crossed Philadelphia Pike. A squad car pulled up for the Officer. Rahmir was cut off by a police van shortly after. They caught him as he came out of an alley.

“Where is it?” The officer that was chasing him asked.

“Where is what?” Rahmir asked irritated.

“The drugs, oh here’s the money, Now where is the drugs?” The Officer demanded an answer as he patted Rahmir down.

“Here it is he threw it when you were chasing him.” A second officer said as he walked up.

“Oh so now we have money and drugs. What a shame you won’t be able to play in tomorrow’s game.” The officer said as he chuckled.

“What the fuck?” Rahmir said confused as ever.

“Take him away.” The first officer said.

Hutch was just riding by on his way to his stash house. He saw the officers putting Rahmir in the squad car.

“Damn I have to get his bail money ready. He had a big game tomorrow too. Damn.” Hutch mumbled to himself.

“Say hello to the bad guy, they say I’m a bad guy. I come from the bottom but now I’m mad fly.” Jay-z came through the speakers of Hutch’s phone.

"What's up T-Roy?" Hutch answered.

"Man, police rolled up on us out here. They never come through." Troy responded out of breath.

"I saw the police putting Rahmir in the squad car. I was wondering what happened." Hutch responded.

"Yeah Old Head, now I got to go back and try to find where I threw that work at." Troy responded.

"If you can't find it then don't worry about it. I'm glad you got away. Rahmir had a game tomorrow though. I'm going to see if they let him post bail tomorrow." Hutch responded.

"Damn, I know he's mad right about now. I forgot all about that game. I heard a scout was supposed to be there to see him play." Troy responded.

"Yeah it was. But I'll holler at you tomorrow. I got to figure out what my next move is." Hutch responded.

"Ok Old Head." Troy responded as he hung up.

Hutch went inside the house where he stashed everything and just sat there thinking. After twenty minutes Hutch's phone interrupted his thoughts.

"Say hello to the bad guy, they say I'm a bad guy. I come from the bottom but now I'm mad fly." Jay-z came through the speakers.

"What's up Styles?" Hutch answered.

"Dude said he wants 100 pounds yo, Can you handle that order?" Styles asked.

"Tell him to meet me at Checkers. I got eighty for him. He can either take that or leave it." Hutch responded.

“All right what day and time should I tell him?” Styles asked.

“Tell him tomorrow, my youngen just got popped. He had a game tomorrow too. I got to find out what’s up with him, when he can post bail.” Hutch responded.

“All right my dude.” Styles responded before he hung up.

“Damn, it’s just too much going on right now. I need to relax right now and gather my thoughts. My next move has to be my best move with Juice. Rahmir career might be down the drain because of me. I need a drink.” Hutch thought to himself.

The next day Hutch went to the police station to see if he could bail Rahmir out. It was Saturday so Rahmir couldn’t see the judge until Monday morning. Hutch knew that already but still figured he’d give it a shot anyway.

After Hutch left the police station, he made arrangements to meet with Juice at six o'clock that evening. Styles agreed to go with him just in case this was a set up. Juice had turned Wilmington upside down trying to kill Hutch. So no one knew what his motives were for trying to squash the beef between Hutch and himself. Hutch second guessed his decision to only take Styles with him. He took ten other people with him to make the transaction.

When six o'clock rolled around Hutch called Styles to see if he was ready to go. He had everyone else with him already.

"Everyday I'm hustling, everyday I'm hustling." Rick Ross came through the speakers of Styles phone.

"Yo what's up Hutch, You ready?" Styles answered.

"Yeah I'm ready, I don't know if this is a set up or what. But make sure you're strapped and come on." Hutch responded.

"All right my dude." Stlyes answered before he hung up.

After ten minutes Styles finally showed up to Hutch's house. They all followed behind each other three cars deep to Checkers.

When they finally made it to Checkers, Juice was about to pull off until he spotted Styles in one of the cars.

Juice was by himself, but Hutch wasn't taking any chances. No one could blame him after the beef him and Juice had.

"What's up Styles? Why are y'all so deep? I said I wanted to squash the beef and do business." Juice asked.

"Yeah, Nigga I thought this was a set up. You tried to kill me remember? You killed

Starsky, and my cousin Eric. You shot my young buck Son. I mean what you don't remember none of this shit? Why wouldn't I come deep?" Hutch said in a bitter tone.

"I know I apologize for all of that. But you have to see my point of view in all of this. I had that Project on lock before I got booked. I felt like y'all should've asked permission to hustle out there. I felt like y'all just stepped on my toes like I was never coming home or something." Juice explained.

"Man look, when you go to jail your spot don't stay reserved unless your right hand man is still holding it down. You went to jail, your right hand is dead and all your people got booked. So how did you assume you still run things in Riverside?" Hutch asked not really wanting to have this conversation.

"Look we both have different points of views on this, but I'm trying to squash this and do business can we do that?" Juice asked cutting the small talk.

"Do you have fifty grand for me? I only have 80 pounds for you." Hutch asked wanting to get this over with.

"Yeah, do you want to count it?" Juice asked.

"Of course I want to count it, examine it to make sure the bills are not counterfeit and everything." Hutch responded.

"You don't want to do that in this parking lot do you?" Juice asked almost hysterical.

"No we're going to go somewhere else." Hutch said in an as a matter of fact tone.

"Follow us." Styles joined in the conversation.

"Ok right behind you." Juice said as he got in his car.

They went to an abandoned house nearby. So Hutch could count the money and Juice could weigh his product.

Hutch, Juice, and Styles went inside while everyone else stayed outside. Hutch finished counting the money and it was all there. They waited for Juice to finish weighing his product. When everything was ok they parted ways.

"It was nice doing business with you partner." Juice said as he was about to leave.

"I'm not your partner but hit Styles up when you need to re up." Hutch responded dryly.

"All right no problem I'll be calling soon. B more loves me." Juice responded before he walked out the door.

After Juice got in his car and drove off. Hutch started making his plot against him.

"This dude is bold and stupid. The next time he calls you let me know. I'm going to take his money again and then rock him." Hutch said as he laughed like an evil genius.

"Dude has to have something up his sleeve. This can't be this easy. It was hard trying to kill this guy, now he's putting himself out there." Styles responded.

"Yeah I know that's why we are going to meet him at checkers again. But this time it's only going to be me and you there. Everybody I got outside right now will be in here in the cut in case that dude is up to something." Hutch responded.

"I like your style Hutch, I like your style. After this you can relax and stop putting that bullet proof on." Styles responded.

"I'll never take this off, just in case I get another dude like Juice coming at my neck, come on let's get out of here." Hutch responded.

Chapter Six

The Jump Off

Sunday finally came and Tamia used every excuse to get out of the house. She had every intention of keeping her date with Cocoa. She felt like she needed this. Sanaa's jealousy was starting to get to her. She wasn't going to cross the line and be with Cocoa sexually until she broke up with Sanaa. She did have that much respect for her but she also wanted to see what else was out there. Tamia had only dealt with men. Sanaa was her first girlfriend which turned out to be a fatal attraction.

"Sanaa I'm going out for a little while. I need to clear my head. Since you've been in the hospital I haven't had time to myself. The situation with Ice is still on my mind. Then the shootout we had with Shawn. Not to mention having to hold the shop down, while you here in the hospital. I need to get out I need some alone time. I'll be back in a little while do you want anything from the store or something?" Tamia said trying to convince Sanaa to let her go out alone.

"Well, all right Mia I guess it'll be Okay. I did want to spend some time with you though." Sanaa responded trying to sound sad.

"We can do that tomorrow Sanaa, I need some alone time now." Tamia said as she walked out the door.

Tamia thought it would be a lot harder to get out of the house than that but she did it. She was on her way to meet Cocoa and she was excited about it.

Cocoa lived in Mt. Airy so it took Tamia about forty minutes to get to her house. When she pulled up Cocoa was in the doorway. Tamia hadn't seen such a beautiful Chocolate woman that was thick in all the right places. That is until she pulled up in front of Cocoa's house. In the strip club Cocoa was wearing a wig and a lot of makeup. You couldn't really tell her natural beauty. But that's what a stripper does sometimes when they don't want to be recognized by a familiar face.

Cocoa locked her front door then slowly made her way seductively down the steps to Tamia's Escalade.

Tamia watch her as the heel of her shoes touched every step. She could see every muscle in Cocoa's calves from the front of her.

Cocoa had on a sundress that nicely shaped her curvy body and round butt. She let out her hair which was very long jet black and wavy. Cocoa's skin was so smooth she didn't need any make up on at all. The first thing that came to Tamia's mind was why is this beautiful woman stripping for a living? She should be a model.

"Hello sexy, I couldn't wait to see you." Cocoa spoke as she got into Tamia's Escalade.

"Hi beautiful, I couldn't wait to see you either. You know you should be a model right?" Tamia responded as she was mesmerized by her beauty.

"A lot of people say that, but that's not what I want to do for a living. I don't want to rely on my looks to get me through life. I mean, I'm not knocking any of the models who are modeling for a living. But to each his own." Cocoa responded.

"Well, you shouldn't rule it out. You could do it part time and do something else full time. I'm just letting you know how beautiful you are." Tamia responded.

"Thank you. I can say the same about you. Why haven't you pursued a career in modeling? You are just as gorgeous as I am." Cocoa responded returning the compliment.

"Like I told you before my partner and I were best friends. We decided to open a salon together when we were like sixteen years old. One thing lead to another and here I am." Tamia explained leaving out her street life.

"Ok fair enough, what movie are we going to go see?" Cocoa asked changing the subject.

"Madea Goes to Jail, it looks like it's going to be funny. I love Tyler Perry's work that dude is very talented." Tamia responded.

"Yes he is, I definitely agree with you on that. I try to catch every one of his plays." Cocoa responded not hiding the fact that she was happy with Tamia's movie selection.

The rest of the ride to the theater they listened to music. Neither one of them wanted to seem too talkative. When they pulled up to the movie theatre the line was so long it was out the door.

"Thank God I used Fandango." Tamia said with a chuckle.

"You're smart I like that already. That's one cool point you earned." Cocoa said with a smile.

"Just one that's all I get? Well I guess I'll have to work on more. I'll have ten by the time the night is over." Tamia said in a charming manner.

"We'll see." Cocoa said as they got their tickets and headed for their movie.

They both enjoyed the movie and afterwards they went next door to Warm Daddies. Tamia didn't want to be gone too long so she took Cocoa home after they ate.

Cocoa had the time she thought she would have with Tamia. She didn't want the day to end, but she also knew Tamia had a girlfriend waiting at home. So she played it cool when Tamia ended the date early. To Cocoa she was a step closer to taking Tamia away from Sanaa.

Tamia felt more relaxed than she had been over the last six months. She enjoyed Cocoa's company so much, that she was already planning their next date while she was taking her home.

When they pulled up in front of Cocoa's house it was eight o'clock. Tamia leaned in to kiss Cocoa and she didn't pull away. That was the most intense kiss either one of them had in a very long time. Tamia hated to pull away but she had to get home to Sanaa. They hugged, said their goodbyes, and Tamia was on her way home.

About forty five minutes later Tamia was walking in the door of her apartment. Sanaa was sitting on the couch with the television off, and no music playing.

"Why are you sitting here in the dark?" Tamia asked.

"I'm just doing some thinking that's all. You needed some you time and so did I." Sanaa said sarcastically.

"I told you we could spend some time together tomorrow. I needed this today. Come on Sanaa don't start with me right now ok. It's your fault anyway. If you weren't tripping so much being all jealous, I wouldn't have needed time to myself." Tamia responded picking up on the sarcasm.

"I apologized for that. How long are you going to hold what I did to Ice against me? I did save our lives when Shawn came to kill us remember?" Sanaa pleaded her case.

"So you think I can just get over all of this without taking some time to collect my thoughts? I handled the situation at the time because I had no choice. Now that I had a minute to breath I needed to do this." Tamia explained.

"You think I'm stupid don't you? I know you were out with someone else. I just don't know whether it was a male or female." Sanaa continued to argue.

"What makes you assume that I was with someone?" Tamia asked not trying to seem like she was getting defensive.

"It's just that woman's intuition I guess." Sanaa responded sarcastically.

"Well like I said I was getting some me time in. I went to the strip club for an hour before I came home." Tamia lied to Sanaa for the very first time.

"Oh you were huh? So you rather go look at other girls than to spend some time with me? Is that what you are telling me? I did just come home from the hospital a few days ago." Sanaa snapped and tried to get some sympathy at the same time.

"You are well enough to do hair so don't try that guilt trip with me. Besides I'm always with you and now that I wanted to relax without having you around it's a problem. We work together, we live together. I mean damn don't you want to be by yourself some times? Maybe that's why you're getting so possessive and crazy, because we're spending all of this time together. Ice was the last straw Sanaa. If you don't calm this jealousy, fatal attraction shit down I'm going to have to leave you alone as much as it'll hurt the both of us. I'm fed up with that shit Sanaa. Everything else about you I love and adore but that shit is enough to drive me away from what I love. Can you understand that?" Tamia finally got what she was trying to say for a while now off of her chest.

"How long have you been feeling like this Tamia? How long have you been thinking about leaving me?" Sanaa asked with tears in her eyes.

"Sanaa look, how many times have I told you about your jealousy, at first I thought it was cute but now it is too far out of control, it's fatal now. You killed someone because you thought he was going to take me from you." Tamia responded. Not falling for the sympathy card Sanaa was trying to throw.

"Look Mia, I said I was sorry. I can't promise you anything but I'll try to control myself. I understand what you're trying to say and I'm going to work on my Jealousy if it'll save our relationship." Sanaa compromised.

"Thank you because we have too much invested to end this with us. I know if I leave you'll want to sell the shop and really be done with each other. Being friends after we split up wouldn't be good for either of us because the love is still there. I will admit I wasn't at a strip club tonight. I was out with someone I met last week at the strip club. I had to come clean because I felt bad about keeping it from you because I never lied to you before. I want to work this out with you Sanaa."

"Did you sleep with her?" Sanaa asked not really wanting to know the answer if it was bad.

"No I didn't we caught a movie and dinner. I did give her a kiss goodbye though. I will admit that. I'm sorry but I felt like I needed to go out with someone else. I love you and don't want to lose you but I won't tolerate your jealousy." Tamia admitted.

"The thing is everything in me wants to go out with someone else to get even for you doing it. But I don't want to be with anyone but you. So I'm going to working on me to save my relationship instead." Sanaa responded.

"Ok, come here. Give me a hug." Tamia responded.

"Can we start over? Starting tonight?" Sanaa asked with a cute puppy look on her face. Tamia never could resist it.

"I guess so, yes we can start over." Tamia responded as she kissed Sanaa good night.

Chapter seven

The Fashion Show

A year later than expected, The Fashion show was approaching in a week and Tamia was more nervous than excited. She had a few families of butterflies in her stomach. That was the first time she had ever felt like that.

"Tamia, Are you excited about your first Fashion Show?" Amber asked.

"I'm a little nervous actually." Tamia responded.

"Girl what do you need to be nervous about? Those styles are the hottest I've seen since Jeans with the leather and suede in the front of them." Keisha added to the conversation.

"Thank you Keisha. I don't know why I'm nervous. I guess it's because this is my first fashion show. I hope all of my models show up." Tamia responded.

"Tamia everything is going to be fine. The models you picked are going to bring out your styles and our hairstyles. You are talented so relax." Sanaa reassured her.

"Thanks Sanaa. I appreciate that. I guess everything will go along smoothly. I hope it's a big turn out." Tamia responded.

"It will be we put out flyers everywhere. The after party is going to be off the chain too. Relax Mia we got you." Sanaa responded.

"Look, Tamia I didn't spend six months creating styles to match your outfits for this to be a disaster. It's going to be a nice turn out." Amber added.

"Just think if skinny jeans were actually something people called fashion. That just means you're going to knock the hinges off the doors to the world of fashion with your styles. But our hairstyles aren't to be slept on either. You are going to be successful at being a designer and we are going to bring the shop more clientele." Keisha also added to the conversation.

"Thanks y'all. What did you put on the flyers Sanaa?" Tamia asked.

"I put: Spoiled Br@ Hair Technicians' First Annual Hair and Fashion Show. Then I put the Location, time, and date. The Fashion Designer is Spoiled Br@'s very own TAMIA. That's just the front and on the back: The official After Party of Spoiled Br@'s hair technicians' First Annual Hair and Fashion Show and the time, Date, and location. Does this meet your approval?" Sanaa asked excited.

Sanaa actually has been behaving herself since her and Tamia had a talk about her jealousy. She has been on her best behavior. Sanaa loved Tamia so much that if Tamia died in a motorcycle accident, she would want to be on the back of the bike. The last thing Sanaa wanted to do was lose the love of her life.

"Yes it is to my liking but I would have liked to see the flyers." Tamia said with a chuckle.

"Well I thought you'd say that so I kept one for you." Sanaa responded as she handed Tamia the flyer.

"Oh this is nice. I like this. You did a great job on this S." Tamia responded. Liking what she saw.

"Are you a little more at ease now, Mia?" Amber asked.

"A little bit. I'm still nervous some though." Tamia responded.

“I still don’t think we should’ve closed the shop for this week though. We could still be making money right now. All of our hairstyles are ready to go and so are your clothes. We only need two days to do the models hair not a whole week.” Keisha added to the conversation.

“Well, Miss Money Hungry you just wait until the clientele start pouring in for you. After this show people will really see your work. So be prepared for the increased clientele, Oh and you too Amber.” Tamia responded.

“Yeah then you two will be eating like us. We closed the shop to mentally prepare ourselves also. I know it’ll take two days to do all of the models hair. The shop also needs cleaning that’s why we are here while it’s closed. I was thinking we would make it spotless and take some pictures. Maybe form our own hair magazine with our hairstyles in it. We can also do some features from Tamia's clothing line." Sanaa added her Ideas to the conversation.

"We may need to expand too. I saw a building on the East side that's available. We might be able to find a building outside of Chester, you know put one in another city." Tamia suggested.

"That sounds like a good idea but who's going to run it? We're going to need a few more Hair Technicians to pull that off. It's just the four of us." Keisha added to the conversation.

"That's not a problem. I'll run one shop and Sanaa will run the other. We'll hire more Hair Technicians for both shops. I like that you are using the proper terminology for what we do." Tamia replied with a smirk on her face.

"But I like working with the two of you and Keisha. I don't want to split up." Amber interrupted with her wining.

"We enjoy working with the two of you too. But you don't understand how this fashion Show will affect the clientele. There are a lot of guys out there who don't know we cut men's hair. There are a lot of women out there who don't know about this shop. This Fashion Show will reach out to those people also not just our current clients." Tamia explained.

"Exactly, do you want to eat or what? It's not like you will not be able to see us. Maybe we will take turns with what shop we'll be at or something. Maybe we could still all come back to working together after we hire more staff." Sanaa added trying to comfort Amber.

"Ok in that case I'm cool with it." Amber responded.

"I can't wait I'm trying to push big whips like y'all two." Keisha said excited.

"Well you two know it's not going to happen overnight right? After this shop starts over flowing with customers then we'll open another one." Tamia spoke as she made her way to her office.

"We know." Keisha shouted.

All week long the girls prepared for the show. When the day finally came a few of the models were late. Tamia panicked at first but she figured out a way to pull it off. The ones who were late she just worked them in last.

The show was a success. A lot of well known people from the Tri State area attended the Fashion Show. There were a lot more people there than any of the girls expected there would be.

The after party had an even better turn out than the show. The bouncers had to stop letting people in, it was so jam packed inside. Tamia, Sanaa, Amber, and Keisha all had a ball at the after party. They popped bottle after bottle celebrating the turnout of both the Show and the After Party.

A few guys decided to buy a few bottles of their own. That was their way of getting closer to the girls. They figured in order to ask one of them out, they needed a big bank roll and had to show it. None of the guys were cute, so none of the four girls were interested. Just as Keisha told them just that, Cocoa walked over to their table in the V.I.P with a bottle of her own.

Cocoa was very upset that Tamia never called her after their date. She thought everything was fine between them. The chemistry was there and the kiss proved it. So of course Cocoa wanted to know what happened.

"Hello ladies, congratulations on the success of your show. You ladies have skills those hair styles were tight. Tamia I can't wait until that clothing line comes out."

Cocoa greeted the ladies as she took a seat at the table next to them.

"Thank you." All four women said in unison.

"You definitely know taste when you see it, I like that." Sanaa responded.

"I most certainly do Sanaa, that is your name right?" Cocoa responded.

"Yes it is and your name?" Sanaa asked.

"Oh I'm Cocoa, It's so nice to meet you ladies, and you two are Keisha and Amber right?" Cocoa responded.

In the back of Tamia's mind she was wondering what in the hell was Cocoa up to. She knew she had a girlfriend and she also knew her name. So what was this stunt she was trying to pull? As if she left on a bad note. The reason she hadn't called Cocoa was because she wanted to give

Sanaa a chance to change. But what Cocoa was up to made Tamia's head spin.

"Yeah I'm Keisha and she's Amber." Keisha added to the conversation.

"Four beautiful and talented ladies it's hard for me to choose a stylist. But Tamia do you have room in your busy schedule to take on a new client?" Cocoa asked.

"Actually I do. I never turn down money. Here's my card just call the shop and make an appointment." Tamia responded trying to hurry Cocoa along.

"Why thank you. I have a few friends that are interested in coming to your shop to get their hair done as well. They should be here shortly. The rest of you are about to get new clients too." Cocoa responded playing her hand very well.

"I surely have room for more clientele. As a matter of fact I need to start handing out my business cards right now." Amber responded as she excused herself.

"Yeah so do I, wait up Amber." Keisha added.

"I think they just got motivated." Tamia said.

"Yup, they sure did. They went from celebrating to promoting in a matter of minutes." Sanaa responded.

"So Cocoa were your friends at the show with you or no?" Sanaa asked.

"They were but they made a stop before coming here. They might not be able to get in." Cocoa responded with a smirk.

"Oh and why is that?" Sanaa asked.

"Because they aren't letting anyone else in unless a few people leave. And from the looks of things that'll never happen any time soon." Cocoa responded.

“Oh, so how are they going to meet us if they don’t get inside the club?” Sanaa asked.

“Well if they don’t I’ll just have to bring them to the shop when I have my appointment.” Cocoa answered.

“Ok I guess you have this all figured out then huh?” Tamia asked adding to the conversation.

As jealous as Sanaa was, it was surprising that she didn’t flip out. Something didn’t seem right to Sanaa. But she knew if she caused a scene in the club Tamia would be upset. It took everything in Sanaa not to be her old self and curse Cocoa out.

“So Cocoa, tell me how did you and your girlfriends end up split up if you all were at the Fashion Show?” Sanaa asked getting very suspicious of Cocoa’s motives.

"I met them there because I was running a little late. My boss held an unexpected meeting with me and my co workers." Cocoa answered.

"And what is it that you do for a living?" Sanaa asked.

"Oh I'm a stripper part time. I'm also a full time student. This is my last semester. I'll have my Bachelor's Degree in Business. I might just go for the money and go on to get my Master's Degree." Cocoa answered trying to rub her degree in her face.

"Oh really well congrats on your graduation. What club do you strip at?" Sanaa asked.

"I strip at club Tonyx. It's an upscale strip club. It's not your average hood strip joint. A lot of Stars be there. You can catch anyone from Porno Stars to Rappers. " Cocoa answered. She felt as though she would be a better mate for Tamia than Sanaa.

"Oh so you degrade yourself in style huh? I take it you're Diamond from Player's Club of the Tri State huh?" Sanaa replied sarcastically as she was picking up on Cocoa's cattiness.

"Sweetheart stripping is not degrading. I don't have sex for money. I create a fantasy for Men and Women who don't get that kind of attention at home. Isn't that right Tamia?" Cocoa asked catching Tamia off guard.

"Oh so Mia you know this Bitch huh?" Cocoa asked.

"Yeah we met at her job and the female I told you I went out with was her. I haven't called or spoken with her since then I promise you that. I didn't want to lose what we had and all that we have invested in this relationship so I didn't take it any further than that. I told you all of this I just didn't say what her name was." Tamia explained.

"So what the fuck is this all about? If Tamia hadn't talked to you since y'all little date, why the fuck are you up here trying to act like a fucking stranger or something? I will beat the shit out you over her. And by the way she is not doing your hair. I'm not going to create a scene and put you on your back but I suggest you leave and stay the fuck away from my pussy." Sanaa said with some authority in her voice.

"For now I will, but I hadn't had any of your pussy yet. But I'm determined to get a taste of it and besides I'm better for her anyway. You should relax after Tamia leaves you we'll give you a threesome with us if you act right." Cocoa responded disrespectfully as she walked away.

"Tamia, you know it took everything in me to not whip her ass in this club. Do you see how much I've changed? And one more thing sweetheart if I find out you fucked that bitch I'm going to beat your ass." Sanaa responded through clinched teeth.

"Look she just told you we didn't. Now her disrespectfulness is because you have something that she wants so don't let it get to you. I was wondering what she was up to." Tamia responded.

"Yeah I bet you were and by you not telling me that was the bitch you went out with. You made yourself look suspect." Sanaa said as she walked off to mingle with the crowd who weren't in the V.I.P.

"I don't believe this bitch had the nerve to come over here like that. How the hell did she find out about the Fashion Show and this party anyway?" Tamia thought to herself.

When Cocoa seen Sanaa storm off she made her way back over to where Tamia was. Tamia was not thrilled to see her come back over to her. She was hoping Sanaa didn't see her because she knew the outcome already.

"First of all you were very disrespectful. Second, I don't even want to be near you right now. Third, if you ever talk to my girl like that again I will kick your ass myself. She already wants to do it. Now if you'll excuse me I'm going to go mingle." Tamia said as she angrily walked away.

"You say that now. Wait until I taste that pussy you'll be singing a different tune then." Cocoa shouted before she finished her bottle of Champagne. Afterwards she left the club.

Tamia made her way over to Sanaa to reassure her that nothing happened. The last thing Tamia wanted was her already jealous girlfriend to become even worst by assuming she cheated.

"Look S I told you ever thing that happened between me and her. Yes I was wrong for going out with her but I explained to you why I did it. I never lied to you before so why should I start now? I love you so calm down. I didn't say anything at first because I wanted to see what she was up to, because I told her about you from the jump so she knew who you were. I just don't believe after one date she would act like that. Now I wonder if she has a fatal attraction." Tamia explained hoping Sanaa would understand.

"Who wouldn't have a fatal attraction to you Tamia. You see how you got me." Sanaa responded now feeling a little buzzed and horny from the champagne.

"I love you but I don't need anyone else that acts like you." Tamia joked but was dead serious.

"I am a changed woman as you saw tonight. She was begging for me to act a fool but I didn't. I rather let her be petty than to lose my baby. I'm feeling horny let's go home Mia." Sanaa responded.

"Make up sex, Make up sex it's the best sex of the year girl." Tamia sang changing the words to Jeremiah's song.

"Yes the best sex we have besides when you're feeling naughty." Sanaa said seductively.

"I'm always feeling naughty, so we always have the best sex." Tamia seductively responded.

"Exactly my point let's go make love." Sanaa responded.

"Say no more. Let's go before anyone sees us leaving." Tamia said as she grabbed Sanaa's hand and headed for the back door of the club.

Chapter Eight

Prom Night

Finally, Troy's prom night came around. Hutch was actually more excited than Troy was. This brought back memories for Hutch. He went to the prom for three years in a row when he was in High School. He looked dapper at every last one of them too. He had decided to let Troy take his BMW to the Prom. He had so much love for Troy it was crazy. He acted as if Troy was his blood little brother.

"Big things popping, and little things stopping." T.I came through the speakers of Troy's phone.

"Yo, what's up Old Head?" Troy answered.

"I got the beamer detailed for you for tonight young gunner. You need a few extra ones or a hotel room? I know you not eighteen yet so you can't rent one yourself." Hutch asked.

"Nah, I'm cool Old Head. I got a stash and I'm cool on the telly too. Shorty said she not doing anything tonight. We're going to the Prom and probably six flags tomorrow. Can you rent me a car for tomorrow though? I know I can't hold the Beamer to go there." Troy asked.

"No problem youngen I got you. I'm going to holler at you later though. I have to go pick Rahmir up. They finally let my dude post bail." Hutch said as he ended the conversation.

Troy was on his way to get his hair cut. He wanted it fresh for his prom pictures. His

Gucci suit was pressed and laid out on his bed. As well as his shoes and cuff links.

Troy decided to get himself a new watch as well. After he got himself a hair cut it was off to the Christiana mall.

Meanwhile Hutch was on his way to the prison to pick up his protégé. He knew Rahmir would be upset about missing the game. So Hutch decided to wait until he asked about it to tell him they lost. He wanted to wait until he asked about the NFL scout also.

"What's up Old Head? Thanks for picking me up and posting my bail." Rahmir said as he got inside the car.

"No problem Rah. As far as the bail that's how real cats play the game. If you hustling for me and get popped then I have to bail you out it's the rule. Whatever you got caught with, the debt is forgiven that's also the rule. Too bad everybody doesn't play by the rules." Hutch responded.

"Thanks Old Head I didn't know that. I didn't get caught with a lot though I still got two and a half ounces in the tuck. I got caught with a stack and like a stack worth of dope. I'll eat that two stacks and still give you what I owe you. That was my fault if I would've went in the house like I started to, I wouldn't have got caught. I was being greedy." Rahmir responded.

"Yeah, look how about you eat a stack and I'll eat a stack since you insist." Hutch suggested.

"All right bet cause I'm about to get right back out here. Now I know I have to be on point. One of those bastards had the nerve to say to me "I guess you're going to miss your game tomorrow" before he put me in the car. That was a set up my dude. I just don't know who set me up." Rahmir responded.

"Look when you post up, don't post up in the same spot. They're obviously on to that spot." Hutch responded.

"I got two questions. Did we win? And was a scout really there?" Rahmir asked.

"I didn't want to say anything but yeah it was a scout there. And no y'all loss, your team really missed you out there. The school heard about you getting locked up and they kicked you off the team. I tried to tell them it was a miss understanding but they weren't hearing it my dude." Hutch explained.

"Damn, that's what I didn't want to happen. It's cool I'll stack my money up and go to another school. If I stack two hundred and fifty grand I can stop hustling and try to make a run for the NFL since a scout was really there." Rahmir said finally coming half way to his senses.

"That sounds like a plan. You sure you don't want to stop now though. If you get caught again you might not be able to play at another school." Hutch reminded him.

"Yeah but I need to pay my Lawyer so he can beat this case. I threw the work and none of them punk police cats saw me throw it either so it might not even be my work. They setting me up I'm telling you. I know where I threw it and matter of fact take me pass there. I need to get this gwap up for that and so I can fall back while I'm in school." Rahmir responded.

"All right sounds like you got this figured out already. Where did you toss the work at?" Hutch asked.

Take me to the club I tossed it behind there. It's a dumpster I put it behind. The cops took the money. But I doubt that one of them saw me put it there. Did it rain since I was locked up?" Rahmir asked.

"Nah it didn't. So what did they say you were caught with?" Hutch asked now more interested in the case.

"They didn't they just said possession with intent to deliver." Rahmir responded.

"Somebody probably had money on that game. That's the only thing I see why someone would set you up." Hutch said as he pulled in back of A Club Called West.

Rahmir got out and searched for his package. After about fifteen minutes he found it. He was happy he didn't take too much of a loss because of his incarceration.

"See here it goes right here Old Head. I told you this was a set up. They planted that shit on me or picked somebody else's pack up off the ground. It was a lot of heads out there but they chased me." Rahmir said after he got back inside the car.

"This was a set up and this right here proves it. I wonder if Juice had this done or somebody in Riverside is ratting. I didn't get a chance to tell you that Juice stepped to Styles. He told him he wanted to squash the beef and do business. I took his money. But the next time he's a dead man." Hutch responded.

"I don't know Old Head you think it was him. I think we got a rat in the project my dude. He's a wanted man in Riverside. How would he know I play football and I where I hustle at?" Rahmir asked.

"You have to watch everybody out here son. He could've paid some young buck that's not on the squad to give up info. If he ride pass on his bike or something you wouldn't pay attention to him. Think about it." Hutch responded.

"Yeah you're right you do have a point." Rahmir said.

"I can't wait to kill this son of a bitch." Hutch uttered.

"Take me to the strip so I can knock this work off. I have to beat this case and get this gwap up. When I go to the NFL Old Head you're not going to have to hustle no more I promise you that." Rahmir said as they pulled up inside of the project.

"I hear you. You be safe out here my dude. I got to see Troy off to his prom and give him the beamer." Hutch said as he pulled off.

"Damn my dude gets to push the Beamer. I wonder if he'll let me push it." Rahmir said to himself.

"I can't wait until Hutch gets here with the beamer." That's going to top it all off." Troy said to himself.

Troy spent an hour and a half getting dressed. He never looked at himself in the mirror so much before that day. He double checked everything. He made sure he had the tickets, the corsage, and money.

It was five thirty when Hutch finally showed up. The prom started at seven o'clock. He had just enough time to take pictures and pick his date up.

"What's up youngen, you're looking dapper as ever. You look like a young me with that fly shit on." Hutch said as Troy came to the door.

"Thanks Hutch. I'm hype right now. I can't wait to show off my Gucci suit and pulling up in that beamer on top of that is going to set it all off." Troy responded.

"Come on are you ready? You have to drop me back off to my other whip." Hutch asked.

"Yeah hold up my mom wants to take pictures." Troy responded as he went to get her.

After a few minutes Troy came back with his mother. She thanked Hutch for letting her son use his car. She took about twenty pictures before they got inside the car to pull off.

Troy picked up his date after dropping Hutch off to his car. When they got to the prom they definitely were the show stoppers. They felt like they were going to the BET Awards rather than the prom with all of the lights flashing from the spectators taking pictures.

The next day Hutch did as he promised and rented Troy a car to take his prom date to Great Adventures. Troy had the weekend of his young life then it was back to the block he went.

Troy figured he'd get some money during the summer before he went off to College. Troy had a nice amount of money stashed away. He had way more than Rahmir and Troy was only seventeen. He had a good head on his shoulders to be so young.

After graduation Troy spent the whole summer saving up money for school. He didn't want to be like Rahmir and sell drugs while he was in college. Troy had a full Basketball scholarship to a Division one school. He also had an academic scholarship. He would get his degree in Psychology to fall back on if he didn't make it to the NBA.

Rahmir spent his whole summer trying to get into another school to finish his education and his college football career. He beat his case but never found out who set him up. Hutch assumed it was Juice so they went with that thought. Rahmir had saved up over seventy five thousand dollars nowhere near how much he wanted. Three weeks before the semester started he found a school who would accept him.

Troy on the other hand saved up one hundred and fifty thousand dollars. He had stopped selling drugs for Hutch a month before his semester started. Troy wanted to enjoy some of his summer instead of selling drugs all day unlike Rahmir he wasn't addicted to the fast money. Troy did everything he could think of that he didn't get to do while he was busy selling drugs on the strip for Hutch. That consisted of going to the beach with his friends, and going on dates with females of his interest. He knew once school started it was time to get to work.

Chapter nine

First Date turned to stalker

It was a hot summer morning when Tamia woke up from her slumber. She snuck out to get a dozen roses for Sanaa. When Tamia made it back she immediately started breakfast. She was in the dog house and knew exactly how to get out of it.

Sanaa was awakened by the sweet aroma of scrambled eggs, Turkey Bacon, French toast, Grits and Home Fries. Her favorite breakfast combination was staring right at her when she opened her eyes. Tamia had laid out the bedside table with the roses and breakfast on it. Attached to the roses was a card that read: I don't always have the words to say, but I love you. I don't always have the actions to show but, I adore you. I don't always keep my cool but, I hate when we argue. I love you Sanaa and I can't stand when you're mad at me.

Sanaa gave Tamia a big hug, accepted her apology then ate her breakfast. They went on as if it was a routine day. They got dressed after they ate then headed to the shop.

Amber and Keisha were already there as usual. They were hungry and the growth of their clientele showed it. When Tamia and Sanaa walked in all four girls greeted each other. Tamia and Sanaa greeted the clients as well.

About three hours into the day the door open. Tamia was in shock when she saw who walked in. Amber and Keisha thought nothing of it and spoke to the girls. When Sanaa turned around and saw the one face she recognized out of the three girls, she went off.

"What the fuck? I know you didn't just have the nerve to walk up in my shop like I didn't tell you that Tamia wasn't doing your hair. On top of that I told you to stay away from my pussy. You want your ass whipped don't you?" Sanaa angrily shouted as Tamia restrained her.

"Calm down I'm not here for Tamia to do my hair I want one of those two to do it and I brought the two friends I promised them. I always keep my word. Besides Amber and Keisha can do some hair too. This shop does take walk in clientele doesn't it?" Cocoa responded.

"Sanaa, Can you come into the office for a minute? I want to talk to you." Tamia said as she pulled her towards the office door.

"What do you want Tamia I'm not done with this bitch yet?" Sanaa asked angry that Tamia was pulling her away.

"Look Sanaa that's what she wants. She wants to get under your skin and provoke you. You have what she wants. Why do you think she's going out of her way to push your buttons huh?" Tamia asked.

"I guess you have a point, Mia." Sanaa responded.

"So let's go back out here and continue with our day. Besides let Amber and Keisha get that money. Never turn away money this is a business." Tamia responded.

"Ok Mia, I can do that. I'm calm. After all I'm the one waking up next to you every morning. It's me you cooked breakfast in bed for this morning." Sanaa responded.

"That's my girl. Now give me a kiss and come on. We have hair to do." Tamia responded.

“Is everything cool Sanaa? Do you want me to tell them to go to another shop?” Amber asked.

“Yeah because we are loyal to y’all, we’re not going to let a few dollars come between us.” Keisha added.

“No I’m cool. You two go ahead and get that money. Their money is green like everyone else’s.” Sanaa responded with a smirk on her face.

“Oh okay, well in that case which one of you ladies wants to go first? I’m almost done with this client.” Amber asked.

“I’ll go first all I want is a wrap.” Cocoa responded upset Sanaa didn’t take the bait.

Amber took two of the girls and Keisha took the other one. The whole time Cocoa and her friends were in the shop Tamia and Sanaa didn’t pay them any attention. They were laughing and joking like they normally do with Keisha and Amber.

Sanaa told Amber and Keisha about the breakfast Tamia had cooked for her. They finally were open with them and their clients about their relationship. To their surprise everyone accepted it.

As Cocoa listened to Sanaa speak about her morning with Tamia she was sick to her stomach. She wanted that to be her so bad she couldn't stand listening to their conversation. But she had no choice she was under the dryer. You could see the bitterness in her face.

After that day Cocoa never returned to the shop. Her two friends however were weekly clients for Keisha and Amber. Sanaa had won the first battle and she felt real good about herself. Sanaa was starting to actually change from the jealous person that she's been known to be. Amber and Keisha were enjoying the growth of their clientele. Everything was going just as they wanted it to go.

Spoiled Br@ hair Technicians was scheduled for another Hair and fashion Show in a few months. The clientele grew so much from the last one they decided to have another one. Tamia's line was going to be available for purchase two months after the second Fashion Show so everything was going according to plan. On one of their appointments before the show Sanaa decided to ask questions.

"So tell me why haven't your friend Cocoa been back to let Amber do her hair? I'm quite sure she needs it done by now. She said she was looking for a new Stylist." Sanaa asked one of Cocoa's friends.

"She didn't actually say why she hasn't been back here. I actually haven't seen that much of her since she was here that day. I didn't know she never came back." The Friend responded.

Sanaa spoke too soon the next week she ran into her at the bank. Sanaa was taking the deposit to the bank while Cocoa was opening an account. Sanaa didn't think anything of it. She just thought she spoke her up. From that day forward she would see Cocoa almost everywhere she went. Sanaa only would see Cocoa when she wasn't with Tamia.

After about the tenth time Sanaa ran into her she finally told Tamia. Tamia just thought Sanaa was tripping out. She suggested maybe she moved in the area. That would explain why she always ran into her. Sanaa had a strange feeling she was being stalked.

"You might have won the battle but I'm going to win the war." Cocoa thought to herself as she drove past the shop and saw Sanaa talking to Tamia in between clients.

"Tamia I'm telling you I have a gut feeling that she's up to something. I only see her when I'm not with you. You don't find that strange?" Sanaa asked wanting to get to the bottom of the situation.

"I still think you are over reacting. Why would she be stalking you, when it's me she wants?" Tamia asked thinking Sanaa was just paranoid.

"I don't know maybe to try to make me uncomfortable or something. Like how I know she felt when she had to listen to our conversation. I'm glad you pulled me to the side before I reacted to what she was trying to do." Sanaa responded.

"Well good because you lose your cool too fast. You react without thinking and that's not a good thing." Tamia responded.

"What's going on y'all? I mean if y'all got beef with this chick let us know." Keisha asked.

"It's not really beef. Tamia and I were having some problems. Tamia went on a date with this bitch one time then worked on preparing our relationship. She hadn't talked to her since their little date. She felt as though she wanted to pop up at the Fashion Show and After Party. She was even bold enough to come over to us in the V.I.P remember? When y'all stepped off to mingle and promote, this bitch got real disrespectful out of her mouth. I told her Tamia wasn't doing her hair and to stay away from my pussy. Then she showed up here with her two friends. That pretty much sums it up." Sanaa responded.

"Wow, I wonder if she sent her friends in here to spy on y'all. If you keep seeing this bitch when you're not with Tamia, then she might be stalking you. Y'all exchanged words and this bitch is bold enough to come in here and introduced herself at the party. Tamia I think Sanaa is on to something. She feels like her plan back fired." Amber responded.

“See Tamia you think I’m just tripping. I’m not just tripping I’m not tripping at all.” Sanaa responded.

“Well what do y’all think she’s up to? If she feels like she’s going to get me one way or the other why would she stalk Sanaa and not me?” Tamia asked.

“I don’t know but Sanaa you be careful, watch what you say in front of her friends. Tamia you might need to watch your back too.” Keisha responded.

“Watch my back for what? I will beat her into the next day if she tries anything with me.” Tamia responded.

“I’m just saying this bitch is bold. She might be capable of anything. You never know.” Keisha reasoned.”

“All right if you say so, but if she didn’t move down here I know where she lives.” Tamia responded.

"I know where she works. So she can try whatever she likes." Sanaa added.

From that day forward Sanaa walked around like she was being followed. She constantly looked in the rear view mirror when she was driving. She constantly turned around to see who was behind her. Everywhere she seen Cocoa before Sanaa paid extra close attention to her surroundings.

After a month of Sanaa looking around as if she were paranoid she started to calm down. As soon as she did Tamia and Sanaa saw Cocoa at the movie theatre. They acted as if they didn't see her. When they got in the car they had a discussion about it.

Cocoa knew exactly how to play her cards right. She got Sanaa right where she wanted her. Paranoid as ever and then backed off enough for her to put her guard down. Her plan was to torture Sanaa by driving her crazy. If Sanaa reacted the wrong way maybe Tamia would leave her. If that happened she could start dating Tamia again. Cocoa figured she'd tried to fix her relationship when she didn't hear from her after their date. Cocoa was really feeling Tamia and was not taking no for an answer.

The Fashion Show was scheduled to go on in a few weeks. The ladies decided to focus in on that instead of what Cocoa was up to. Tamia and Sanaa wasn't about to let anything stand in their way of their success. They had goals of expanding the shop and opening a clothing store with Tamia's styles as the main line. Cocoa was just a bump in the road they planned on just running over.

Cocoa decided she would keep a low profile until the Hair and Fashion Show. Cocoa was plotting her moves like a game of Chess. She definitely was pulling out all the stops to get what she wanted. How did she find the time to dance and juggle her last semester when school started, Yet still keep close tabs on what Tamia and Sanaa were doing was remarkable. It's not like she had a lot of time on her hands. But Cocoa was determined to get her claws into Tamia one way or another.

Chapter Ten

The Spotlight

Rahmir finally found a school to attend for his last year in college. He had to move to Baltimore, so his days of selling drugs for Hutch were about to come to an end. He didn't have the amount of money he wanted to have by the time he went to school. But he was willing to manage without selling drugs. After all his NFL career was on the line.

Rahmir spent his whole summer selling drugs on the strip. By Mid Summer he had his Lawyer paid up. The rest of the summer he spent saving up money for school and working out. Rahmir had ideas about selling T- Shirts, Hats, under clothes, etc.

Rahmir spent countless hours on the internet looking for wholesalers. He needed to continue his hustle just not with drugs. He was used to a certain lifestyle and planned to keep it that way.

Troy on the other hand was a humble young man. He had enough money to last through his four years of college. Troy wasn't a flashy kind of guy. All he needed he already had. The only thing he was focused on was making it to the NBA.

Rahmir needed the latest designer clothes, the latest sneakers, the latest fitted hats, technology, and game consoles. You name it and he had to be the first one with it. He needed a lot of money in his possession to feel secure.

He needed to get drafted in to the NFL. Because if he didn't then he would make selling drugs his only other career choice. Rahmir was addicted to fast money so making millions of dollars to him is the only other alternative.

When the semester started both Rahmir and Troy were what you call "Big Men on Campus". They both were popular high school athletes. In Rahmir's case he was a popular college athlete now. His reputation followed him from his last college.

Rahmir had two weeks before his first game. He was nervous because he didn't have a lot of time to study his new team's Offensive and Defensive playbooks. He intended to play hard and make the scouts come down to Baltimore to scout him.

His team mates and the coach welcomed him with open arms. They played against Rahmir and didn't have an answer for him on the field. He was one of the top ranked running backs in college football. The Pep Rallies made Rahmir real hyper about the game. He had to call is mentor Hutch and invite him down to see him play.

"Say Hello, to the bad guy, they say I'm a bad guy. I come from the bottom and now I'm mad fly." Jay-Z came through the speakers of Hutch's phone.

"What's up Superstar?" Hutch answered.

"You got it Old Head. Are you coming down here to watch me play my first home game? B-more is not too far out of the Mayor of D-Wares' way is it?" Rahmir asked.

"Nah you know I'll be there. Styles said he's coming too." Hutch responded.

“Ok bet. Did Troy leave for college yet? And did y’all handle Juice yet?” Rahmir asked.

“Yeah he left the day after you did. No, we didn’t get him yet but we will though. You just worry about taking care of business on the field. We got this on smash back here.” Hutch responded.

“Ok, Ok, I know you miss me though. I know I miss that money myself.” Rahmir said.

“Yeah I miss you but business is still business without you Superstar if you need anything let me know.” Hutch responded.

“All right Old Head. I’m out I have to study these playbooks.” Rahmir said before he hung up.

When game day finally came around Rahmir was ready. To his surprise there was a scout there on opening day to see him. He spotted Hutch and Styles immediately after he spotted the scout. Seeing those three made Rahmir's adrenaline pump even more. He was ready to run all over the opponents' defense.

Rahmir's team got first possession. Hutch and Styles started cheering when they saw that Rahmir was returning the kick off. The kick was up in the air and Rahmir was getting in position to catch it. As soon as he secured the ball he took off behind his blocker. After twenty yards of being untouched he was grabbed by a linebacker. Rahmir broke the tackle and changed his speed. He jumped over one defender like he was leaping over a hurdle on a relay race track who tried to make a dive tackle. When he got to mid field the spectators were on their feet. Hutch and Styles were going crazy chanting Rahmir's name. It wasn't long before the home crowd followed Hutch and Styles in their chant. Touchdown the referee signaled and the home crowd went crazy.

Rahmir made an immediate impact on his new team. By the end of the game Rahmir was the most popular student at his new school. His stats were amazing he had three touchdowns, rushed for two hundred and seventy five yards, and had two interceptions. The final score was forty two for the Home Team and fourteen for the Away Team.

After the game Hutch and Styles showed how much they were impressed. They ran straight over to Rahmir the first chance they got. They hoisted him up on their shoulders and began chanting again.

“Rah - mir, Rah - mir, Rah – mir, Rah – mir, Rah – mir, Rah – mir.” Hutch, Styles, and The Home Crowd chanted.

“Yeah this is D E representing baby, Riverside all day.” Styles screamed out during the chants.

The scout was impressed also but he wasn't allowed to approach Rahmir. He could only approach the coach about Rahmir and he did exactly that. After the team took their showers and got dressed the coach came in. He told Rahmir and two other guys to meet him early tomorrow before their first class.

Hutch and Styles waited outside for Rahmir. They wanted to take him out to celebrate. Everyone met up at the local college hang out. The Team, the students who were at the game, along with Hutch and Rahmir all partied until curfew. After all they did have practice in the morning as well as classes.

When Hutch and Styles got back to Delaware it was business as usual. They were waiting for Juice to call for a re up so they could murder him. Hutch decided to call Troy to check on him and to tell him about Rahmir's first game.

"Live your life, oh oh oh, no matter where it might take you just live your life." Rihanna and T.I came through the speakers of Troy's phone.

"What's up Old Head? How is everything?" Troy answered.

"Everything good here as a matter of fact we just came back from seeing Rahmir play in his season opener." Hutch responded.

"Oh yeah did they win? How did he do with his new team?" Troy asked.

"Yeah they won and your boy scored three touchdowns. He had two interceptions and rushed for two hundred and seventy five yards." Hutch said excitedly.

"That's what's up Riverside representing all day baby. I can't wait until my season starts." Troy happily responded.

“When does your season start? You know I’m going to fly to North Carolina to see your first college game boy. I need to see my other superstar in action. How are you adapting to college life playboy?” Hutch asked.

“Well preseason is in October and the season starts the last week in October but we’re practicing now. I’m slowly adapting but it’s cool. My roommate is cool too that was the main thing I was worried about.” Troy responded.

“Oh ok let me know the exact date so me and Styles can book our flights.” Hutch responded.

“All right, tell Rahmir congratulations and can you go check on my mom for me?” Troy asked.

“That’s already been taken care of playboy. You know you’re my youngen plus your mom’s got a fat ass.” Hutch joked.

“Watch that shit Old Head I don’t play when it comes to my mom dukes.” Troy responded the least bit amused.

“I’m only joking but I did go check on her as soon as I got back from B more. She fed a brother as usual.” Hutch responded as he rubbed his stomach.

“All right Old Head I got to go. Be safe out there.” Troy said before he hung up.

One month later, Rahmir was already breaking records at his new school. They were undefeated and the favorites to win the championship. Rahmir had already scored twenty touched downs and rushed for over a thousand yards. They were numbers that players with four years in at the school didn’t even have. The day after the opener the coach told Rahmir and two other students that the scouts from NFL teams were intested in drafting them. That was the spark that gave Rahmir the drive to put up those stats in five games. He was hungry to be drafted to the NFL.

The end of October finally came and it was Troy's turn to show off at his opener. His team was playing against a school that had a point guard from Chester name Tamar on their team. Chester was known for breeding Ball players but not all made it to division I schools but this guy did. Troy was up for the challenge after all he was playing in front of Hutch and Styles. He knew he had to represent Delaware. For some strange reason Delaware didn't like Chester natives so it was sort of a player rivalry game also.

They were ready for Tip Off and everyone was seated. Hutch and Styles managed to get front row mid court seats. The ball was in the air, North Carolina got the tip. The tip went to Troy and he wasted no time setting up the offense. After a few passes UNC scored. Duke took the ball out and Tamar brought the ball up court. Troy tried to guard him and Tamar ended up crossing him over like Allen Iverson did Michael Jordan his rookie season.

Hutch and Styles were upset but encouraged Troy anyway. Troy was embarrassed but didn't let it show. He called for the pick and roll when he got down court. Troy came off the pick and drove to the basket for two points. Duke came back down court to answer. Tamar connected with his Power Forward for an Alley Oop. From that play forward Troy knew he had to play his heart out. He heard about the ball players from Chester but never played against any of them. He knew this would be a long night for him.

The game ended with Duke scoring Eighty Three points and UNC scoring Sixty Eight. Troy's team lost but he scored twenty five points, had ten assists and three steals in the opener. Tamar on the other hand scored Thirty two points, had eight assists, and five steals to end the game. Hutch and Styles told Troy that he played a good game. They told him to keep up the good work. He played great his first game for a freshmen in college.

Later that fall Rahmir took Baltimore to the Championship and won it. He sealed the deal on being Drafted a high pick in the draft. For the rest of his final year in college he went to class, partied hard, and hustled hard. He was the man to see if you needed anything ranging from underwear to timberlands he had it for sale. The Spotlight was on Rahmir his whole year down in Baltimore. Hutch and Styles were impressed when they would go down to visit him.

Troy had a great season with UNC. There were talks about an early entry into the NBA for him. He was so set on graduating college that he paid the rumors no attention. Hutch and Styles told him to take the money and come out of college. But Troy didn't even pay them any attention. He knew that if he got hurt, he would need something to fall back on. He decided to do four years of college then enter the draft. He promised that his stock would be even higher by graduation. He wanted to be picked between one and ten that was where the money was. But no one seen it that way so he decided to make them a believer by working on his game during spring and summer breaks.

By the time the season was over for Troy there were talks again about him entering the draft early. This time they set him to go as high as number twelve. That wasn't satisfying to Troy so he told everyone he would stay in college.

When the year was over The NFL Draft Day came. Ramir went number three in the draft. Of course Hutch, Styles, and Troy were proud of him. Actually the whole state of Delaware were celebrating that one of their own got drafted into the NFL. Troy used that as motivation to work harder to be a top pick in the NBA when his turn came around. That night Hutch took Rahmir, Styles, and Troy to the club to celebrate. Bottles of Champagne were on Hutch all night until they all were smashed.

Troy spent the whole summer working on his game. He didn't post up on the strip like everyone thought he was. He even went down to Chester to play in the summer league at Tri State Fitness Center. Everyone who had game played in that league. He wanted to test his game against the best so he could be thought of as one of the best. After Tamar broke his ankles he had a lot of respect for Chester and Chester's Players.

Chapter Eleven

The Road to Success

Finally the day for Spoiled Br@'s Second Annual Hair and Fashion Show came around. The girls were so excited. They knew they would have a better turn out than the last one, even though the first one was a success. They were looking to expand as well as open the clothing store. All four girls were working hard because of those goals. Amber and Keisha got more involve with the process this time around. One day they hoped their hard work would pay off.

They were hoping to be made partners with Tamia and Sanaa after it was all said and done.

Everything was in place for the start of the show. All of the models showed up at the time they were given. The Deejay was playing music as the people were walking in to take their seats. All of the microphones were on and working. The speakers and lighting were perfect. The models were dressed and ready to go. They were lined up in the order that they were supposed to come down the catwalk.

Tamia came out and started the show the exact time it was scheduled. She greeted the audience and introduced the first model. She described the outfit she had on and announced the stylist that did her hair. She went down the line until she introduced all models. She let the audience have an intermission while the models got changed into their next outfits.

Cocoa took the intermission to unleash her surprise. As soon as the people returned to their seats Cocoa took position. When Tamia came back out on stage all of the lights mysteriously went out. The audience was hysterical and so were all the models. Tamia and Sanaa didn't know what to make of it. Amber and keisha were just trying to keep their composure.

The spotlight came on and Cocoa walked out to "Anything" by Jay-Z. The men in the audience cheered her on as she began to give a strip show they all would never forget. Sanaa was furious but she didn't want to drag her off stage by her hair and make the whole show a disaster. Tamia was more upset than Sanaa was as she had to watch Cocoa destroy her show. As soon as the song went off Tamia walked out and escorted Cocoa off the stage as if it was a part of the show. Sanaa found the power switch and turned the rest of the power back on. Amber got on the microphone and announced that was an unexpected performance by Cocoa and to give her a round of applause. Keisha came out to join Amber. They immediately introduced themselves and started the show back up for Tamia.

Meanwhile, Tamia and Sanaa both started beating the crap out of Cocoa and her accomplices. This wasn't the outcome she expected. Sanaa was enjoying giving Cocoa the beating she so badly wanted to give her at the After Party from the first show. After fifteen minutes Cocoa and her crew gathered themselves and left the show.

Tamia returned to the podium and regained control of the show after she gained her composure. Amber and Keisha returned back stage to find a sweaty and hyper Sanaa. The models in line were hyper as well. This was better than the last show to them they saw a show as well as gave one.

“Please tell me you beat that bitch ass she gone too far now.” Keisha angry said.

“And you know I did. I punished that bitch for real.” Sanaa responded excited.

“That bitch had that shit coming, yes she did. I wish I would’ve been back here to see that shit.” Amber added to the conversation.

“That bitch did, you should’ve seen my Mia though she fought the two bitches she had with her. They couldn’t do anything with my Mia.” Sanaa responded even more excited.

“I’m salty I missed that one.” Keisha responded.

“Yeah I’m salty too.” Amber added.

“You should go freshen up before you have to take the stage it’s almost that time.

We have to go out to show the crowd who the stylists are." Amber reminded Sanaa.

"Oh yeah I almost forgot thank you." Sanaa said before she rushed off to the bathroom.

"I'm salty girl I wanted to get some hits in myself. That was some foul shit she did tonight. Just going to perform without being invited to, like Tamia was going to want her after that." Amber said.

"I know girl me too." Keisha responded.

When Sanaa came back they all waited back stage until the last model took her turn down the catwalk. Tamia announced who the stylists were. After each stylist she announced the models whose hair was done by that stylist. Before long Sanaa, Keisha, and Amber took the stage along with all of the models. They received a standing ovation. Sanaa grabbed the microphone and told the crowd to give it up for the Hostess and designer herself. Tamia took a bow as the crowd went crazy. It was the best turn out of the two shows despite of Cocoa's stunt.

The four girls waited until everyone left to start cleaning up. Tamia counted the money that was taken at the door. When they were done they headed to the After Party. They almost didn't get into their own party it was so packed. Tamia was so excited the first thing she did was buy four bottles of Champagne. Each one of them had a bottle to themselves.

The Deejay gave a shout to Tamia for putting on another great Hair and Fashion Show. The rest of the club agreed with him. The night was going perfect.

Meanwhile Cocoa was at the police station pressing charges on Sanaa for the beat down Sanaa had given her. Cocoa knew everywhere to catch Sanaa, her last name, where she lives and every bit of information she gathered when she was following her.

She said nothing about Tamia because she wanted Sanaa incarcerated and out of her way. She was pulling out all of the stops to get what she wanted. Sanaa had fallen right into her strap.

The next day Tamia and Sanaa were out looking for buildings to open a second shop. They finally found one in Philadelphia right on Broad Street in South Philly. The building had a parking lot and everything. Tamia took the number down and planned to call about it the next day.

When Tamia got up the next morning she called about the building. The man that she spoke with arranged for her to look at the building the following day. Tamia was so excited she woke Sanaa up from her slumber.

“S, wake up baby girl I got some good news.” Tamia shouted.

“What is it that you can’t wait another hour until I get up?” Sanaa anger responded.

“It’s about the building on Broad Street grouchy.” Tamia responded with a chuckle.

“What about it is it still available?” Sanaa responded now wide awake.

“Yes it is and we get to take a look at it tomorrow. He doesn’t want that much down or that much for rent either.” Tamia responded.

“What time tomorrow?” Sanaa responded.

“He said tomorrow morning at nine o’clock.” Tamia responded excitedly.

“Ok let’s get dressed so we can go tell the girls.” Sanaa responded as she jumped out of bed.

“I thought you wanted to sleep for another hour Ms. Grouchy.” Tamia jokingly responded.

“Well you did wake me up with some good news.” Sanaa responded as she ran in the bathroom.

They got dressed and made their way to the shop. Surprisingly they got there before Keisha and Amber. They started making arrangements for the opening of the other shop. Sanaa got on the phone and started ordering equipment. Tamia made a list of products she needed to get from the wholesaler in New York. An hour later the girls finally walked in.

“We have some good news ladies.” Sanaa started the conversation.

“Yup so have a seat because we need to talk.” Tamia added.

“So what’s the good news?” Amber asked as she sat down.

“Yeah what’s all of the excitement about?” Keisha also asked as she took a seat next to Amber.

“Well we went out yesterday to look at buildings for the opening of the second shop. We found one that’s perfect right on Broad Street in South Philly.” Sanaa responded.

“Yup and it has a parking lot and everything. We are meeting the guy tomorrow morning to look at the inside. We may even put up the down payment tomorrow.” Tamia added.

“So who’s going to run it?” Amber asked excitedly.

“We are still discussing that. We don’t know yet. Maybe one of you two could manage it. We haven’t decided yet.” Tamia responded.

“Okay I’m with that. As a matter of fact you could let us both manage it. That’s if, one of you two aren't going to be there." Amber responded.

"Well we can decide that after we put the down payment on it and decorate." Sanaa responded.

"Yeah because I might go to Philly just to get away from Sanaa ass. I think we are spending too much time together." Tamia added as she laughed hard.

"How do you know I don't want to go to Philly to get away from you?" Sanaa asked offended.

"Well you can go I'll stay here. Either way I'm getting rid of you." Tamia said as she laughed again.

"Anyway you two are welcome to come along with us in the morning. That's if you don't have clients. We are going to meet him at nine o'clock." Sanaa said to the girls.

"Okay cool we'll be there, right Keisha?" Amber said excitedly.

"Yeah we'll be there. My first appointment isn't until eleven." Keisha confirmed.

"So it's a date." Sanaa responded.

As soon as the conversation was over a few walk in clients came in. From there on out the girls were busy all day long. They needed the other shop because of the increased clientele. Those fashion shows brought in a ton of new clients. All four girls gained more clients after those shows.

Tamia had planned to open her clothing store shortly after the grand opening of the second shop. Everything was going according to schedule. They were right on pace to have three businesses up and running.

What they didn't know, was that Sanaa was about to be arrested for assault. Cocoa planned this whole thing to a tee. She went to the hospital and got her medical records of that night Sanaa beat her up. She had a fractured jaw, a black eye, and two broken ribs. She took pictures and everything. The police had the report, the medical records and statements from Cocoa's friends. They put out a warrant for Sanaa's arrest. This case wasn't looking good for Sanaa.

The following day they went to look at the building. They liked what they saw so they gave the owner the down payment. He then gave them the lease to sign and a set of keys. Tamia wanted to buy the building rather than lease it but the owner wasn't budging. Since the deal was finished they all headed to the shop to meet their clients. They were so excited that they didn't see the light changing and Sanaa ran a red light in front of a police officer.

When they saw the police lights they didn't panic. After all they didn't have any drugs or guns in the car. As far as they knew none of them had any warrants either. Sanaa pulled the car over. She didn't realize she had run the light until the cop was pulling her over.

"Can I have your License and Registration please?" The Officer asked as he approached the car with his hand on his gun.

"Sure Mr. Officer what seems to be the problem?" Sanaa asked as she gave the Officer her License and Tamia's registration to her Escalade.

"Well you ran a light and if everything checks out you will only get a ticket." The officer responded as he walked back to his car.

"Damn he didn't fall for that sexy voice. He could let me go with a warning." Sanaa said in an angry tone.

This isn't what they needed they all thought. The day was going good now they are being held up from getting to their clients on time. Amber and Keisha were never late before. Sanaa and Tamia's regulars knew to expect them late sometimes. The Officer ran the plate and Sanaa's license. After the results the officer called for some backup. In about fifteen minutes another squad car pulled behind the other Officer's car. The girls started to get concerned when they saw the other car. The first Officer approached the second and they both started towards the Escalade.

The first Officer went to the Driver's side. The second officer went to the passenger's side. They both drew their weapons and asked the girls to step out of the car.

Sanaa took one step outside of the vehicle before she was pulled the rest of the way out. The officer wasted no time slapping the hand cuffs on her. He almost handled her like she was a man.

“Ms. Sanaa Daniels you are under arrest for aggravated assault. We have a warrant for your arrest. You have the right to remain silent. Whatever you say can and will be held against you in the court of law. You have the right to an attorney.” The Officer proceeded to read Sanaa her rights.

“What, who did I assault? What do you mean I have a warrant for my arrest? Are you crazy? This must be some type of miss understanding. Are you sure you have the right Sanaa Daniels?” Sanaa argued as she was escorted to the squad car.

“Do you girls have any weapons or drugs in the car?” The Second Officer asked.

“No we don’t. And what are you placing my girlfriend under arrest for? She didn’t do anything.” Tamia asked.

"I can't disclose that information Ma'am. Could you three ladies please step up on the curb and away from the vehicle?" The Second Officer asked.

"For what?" Tamia Asked.

"I am about to search the car for weapons and drugs." The Second Officer responded.

"Not without a warrant you're not. That's my vehicle and I just told you there is nothing in there." Tamia angrily said.

"Ma'am we have probable cause we don't need a warrant." The First Officer joined the conversation after putting Sanaa in the car.

"What probable cause my truck is legit. I don't have any warrants nor am I under arrest." Tamia angrily argued.

"The driver has a warrant out for her arrest so that gives us probable cause." The First Officer answered.

"No, I don't think so. If she was driving my truck without me in it then you would have probable cause but since I'm here you don't. You need a warrant. I have to get to work and get these girls to work also. If you would excuse us we're leaving." Tamia responded as she got back into the Escalade along with the other two girls.

"Ma'am you can't just pull off. Freeze, Ma'am." The First Officer shouted.

"Let her go. She's not under arrest." The Second Officer suggested.

"This is some bullshit how are they going to just lock me up. How are they just going to pull off?" Sanaa thought to herself.

The girls circled the block to follow the cop car that had Sanaa in it. They followed the car to the precinct. They wanted to find out where she was going. Tamia could only think of Cocoa pressing charges on Sanaa. She didn't find out until later when she tried to bail Sanaa out that she was right.

Chapter Twelve

The Riverside Finale

Styles got the call from Juice saying he wanted to re up on some more Marijuana. Styles didn't tell Hutch right away because they were still celebrating. It's not every day someone you know gets drafted to the NFL. Styles decided to wait a week until the celebrating came down to a minimum.

Rahmir wanted Hutch to be with him when he signed his first NFL contract. He planned on keeping his promise of taking Hutch away from the streets and drug dealing. But Hutch told him that he had business to take care of so he couldn't make it.

"I've been gone for a few days. I have to check on business. I might need to re up. You go ahead and take care of that. Hit me up later." Hutch suggested.

"That's just it man, you don't have to sell that shit no more Old Head we made it. I told you I was taking you with me." Rahmir responded.

"I'm a man Rahmir and men take care of themselves. How is that going to make me feel if my young buck is taking care of me? Huh? I always stood on my own two feet. I appreciate it but I can't let you do that." Hutch said.

"Man listen, I can give you a job or something I wouldn't be taking care of you. You looked out for me now it's my turn to look out for you. You gave me a job when I needed it. Now it's my turn to return the favor. Imagine making the same money you making now or more. Without looking out for the police, stick up boys, Dudes like Juice, Haters, and snitches." Rahmir tried to reason.

"Yeah I know but you have to get established first. You're not going to get your first check right away. Then you're going to have to get a house, and then find a job for me. In the mean time I still have to hustle." Hutch reminded him.

"Alright Old Head you stay safe out here until I come back to get you out of here." Rahmir responded not trying to argue his point any more.

Hutch finally got his point across to Rahmir. They parted ways to take care of their individual business. Hutch checked on his workers and Rahmir flew out the next day to sign his first NFL contract.

"Say hello, to the bad guy they say I'm a bad guy, I come from the bottom but now I'm mad fly." Jay-Z came through the speakers of Hutch's phone.

"What's up Styles?" Hutch answered.

"I got to holler at you playboy where are you?" Styles responded.

"I'm on the strip but I'll be at the spot in ten minutes come through." Hutch answered.

"Okay I'll meet you there." Style said before he hung up.

Hutch collected his money from all of the guys he had on his payroll. He had just enough product left to give them all another package. He was almost out of marijuana and cocaine. It was time for him to re up. Only this time he was buying some real major weight for both products. In the State of Delaware Hutch was the man. He started out as a look out and now he was a

Kingpin. That was every career drug dealer's dream, to become a Kingpin.

Ten minutes had gone by and Hutch was not at his Stash house yet. Styles got there in eight minutes but knew Hutch's ten minutes usually meant a half an hour. Just as Styles was about to call Hutch again to see where he was he pulled up.

"Damn man what took you so long you said ten minutes?" Styles angrily asked as he got out of his car.

"I had to collect my money and take inventory out here. I'm here now, what's up?" Hutch asked.

"I'll tell you in the house." Styles said as he got within ten feet of Hutch.

After they entered the house Hutch went straight to his product. He wanted to see exactly how many packages he had available for his workers. Styles followed him so he can tell him the news.

"I got a phone call from your boy last week. He said he needs to re up with you. They love that weed down in B More. He said if you can swing it he needs two hundred pounds this time around." Styles began the conversation.

"He called last week, why the fuck are you just now telling me?" Hutch asked angrily.

"Because he called the day Rahmir got drafted. Everybody was having a good time so I decided to wait." Styles explained.

"Oh you decided? I still could've killed that nigga and celebrated afterwards. Don't make another decision for me for the rest of your life my man." Hutch said displeased with Styles.

"Well what do you want me to tell him? Because he called again today and I told him I'd hit him back in a few hours after I talked to you." Styles asked.

"You call that nigga back and tell him to meet us at the spot we took him to. Tell him I can swing that, I'll see him in four days." Hutch responded.

"All right man, I got you. I'll hit him up after I go pick this change up." Styles responded on his way out the door.

Hutch began to start getting his packages together that he planned on giving to his workers. Afterwards he made a few phone calls to his connects. Hutch found out that he would be without any product for two days. The packages he was about to give out was it for both products.

"Damn, I knew I shouldn't have celebrated with Rahmir for a whole week. I should've been called my Connects for my re up. I never been without work the whole time I was hustling." Hutch thought to himself.

Hutch left his stash house to hand out the packages. In the meantime Styles was picking up his money from the dealers he had under him. It took Hutch two hours to hand out his packages. By the time he got back to his workers they already had more money waiting for him. Hutch decided to tell each and every one of them that he had to wait on his connect for two days. They were disappointed that he was out of product. But what were they going to do it was a part of the game.

"Say hello to the bad guy they say I'm a bad guy, I come from the bottom, but now I'm mad fly." Jay-Z came through the speakers of Hutch's phone.

"What's up Styles?" Hutch answered.

"Juice said okay he'll be there." Styles Answered.

"All right I'll be ready for him." Hutch responded.

After Hutch hung up he called his army. They had a meeting three hours later to discuss what the plan was. They all knew that it was a plot to kill Juice. They just didn't know how it would be executed. After a few hours of plotting and planning they came up with the perfect plan. They covered every scenario and every detail. They even did a few practice runs so everyone would be ready for show time.

After two days Hutch received his order for twenty kilos and 400 pounds of marijuana. He and Styles took the time to break everything down in to packages to hand out to their workers. They were excited to receive the fresh batch. They also knew their customers would be pleased with it also.

It was a half of a day until show time. Hutch decided to rest up until then. Hutch had a long past few days. He barely got any rest so he decided to catch up. He didn't want fatigue to set in just in case Juice was plotting the same thing. This may be a trap for him just like he's trying to set a trap for Juice.

It was one hour until Show Time. Hutch gathered all of his people and had them in place. He was just waiting on Styles to get the call. Hutch didn't have the product Juice wanted with him. He hadn't planned on letting Juice get out of that abandoned house alive. His thoughts were what was the point in making the exchange? He was going to take Juice's money and kill him anyway.

"Push it to the limit, I'm pushing it, I'm pushing it, I'm pushing it, You got to push it to the limit." Rick Ross came through the speakers of Styles's phone.

"What's up Soldier?" Styles answered.

"You player, Is your man ready for me?" Juice asked.

"Yeah pimping he been ready just waiting on you." Styles responded.

"All right I'll be there in an hour." Juice responded.

Styles phoned Hutch to tell him the news. He also wanted to tell him that he was on his way. Styles was still mentally preparing himself for what was about to go down before Juice called him. Styles showed up at the house twenty minutes after he talked to Hutch.

"I'm so glad that you could join us. Wait outside for Juice until he gets here." Hutch ordered.

"What do you want me to do when he get here?" Styles asked.

"Didn't we go over this like fifteen times? It's always the retarded one that gets everybody caught up." Hutch responded.

“Man, shut up and just tell me again.” Styles responded not liking the comment.

“Let that nigga walk in first. I will be looking out the window. I’ll know when he pulls up or walks up whatever.” Hutch responded.

“All right so I get him from behind right? Put the gun to his head and check him for any weapons.” Styles asked.

“By George I think he’s got it.” Hutch responded.

“Yeah all right Hutch.” Styles responded as he went outside to wait for Juice.

Juice showed up five minutes early. His plan was to get his product and head immediately back to B More. He greeted Styles as he got out of the car. Styles spoke back and proceeded according to plan.

“It’s open go ahead in he’s already inside waiting for you.” Styles suggested.

“All right I didn’t know he was here already. I’m used to my Connects always being late.” Juice responded.

Styles laughed as Juice opened the door to go inside. To all of their surprise Juice was alone again. The same man that tore Wilmington up trying to kill Hutch is traveling alone. This dude really does have a lot of balls. Juices’ back must have been against the wall if he’s putting himself out there like this.

“What a way to get caught with your pants down.” Hutch thought to himself.

Styles already had his gun cocked before Juice arrived. He put it to his head and checked for weapons. Juice did have a gun on him. Styles took that and asked if he had any more as he proceeded to check.

“What is all of this? Y’all didn’t check me the last time.” Juice asked.

"I know but two hundred pounds is a lot to get robbed for don't you think? I mean you did bring a gun with you so you feel the same way." Hutch asked.

"Yeah but I always carry my heat with me." Juice responded.

"That's it Hutch that's all he had was this one, that's shocking to see the man who tore Wilmington upside down trying to kill my man." Styles interrupted with a chuckle.

"All right well is that the money right there? Or do you need to go get it?" Hutch asked.

"It's right here every dollar. Now where is my two hundred pounds at? Is that here or do you have to go get it?" Juice responded with the same sarcasm.

"Oh it's right here playboy." Hutch responded as he pulled out his gun and cocked it.

"What's this is this how you do business home boy. Y'all young bucks got the game fucked up. How are you going to rob somebody that's bringing you this kind of paper?" Juice responded.

"That's just it Home Boy. This isn't a robbery. No in fact this is the last words you will utter. This is for my cousin and my dead partner." Hutch said before he squeezed the trigger.

Juice didn't get another word out before he was shot ten times. Hutch emptied the clip on Juice. Styles didn't even get a chance to pull out his badge and say freeze.

The swat team entered the abandoned house from every angle. Hutch and his entourage had nowhere to run. The police had been on to Hutch since he became large in the drug business. They knew about the beef with Juice but could never catch Juice. Now they had them both one was about to be in a body bag and the other one in cuffs. Hutch couldn't understand how someone who grew up in the projects be an undercover police officer. How did he go to the academy and move up in rank without anyone knowing he was a cop? That was a question Hutch's whole crew wanted answered.

"How did such a beautiful run in the game end up like this? It's over for me this dude knows everything and saw me commit a murder. I know I'm getting life." Hutch said to himself as they put him in a squad car.

Chapter Thirteen

The Sweet Taste of Revenge

"Who the fuck pressed charges and got a warrant put out on me?" Sanaa thought to herself.

"Cocoa, it had to be Cocoa. I hate a bitch like that. She threw rocks at an ass whipping and now she's pressing charges on me?" Sanaa continued to think.

"I know Mia is going to bail me out. She probably dropped them off at the shop first." Sanaa still continued to think.

Meanwhile Tamia was at the desk already trying to bail Sanaa out. Lucky for her they locked her up in the morning so she'll get to see a judge in a few hours. Sanaa would be able to get a bail hearing at about three o'clock. She didn't want to sit around the police station waiting so Tamia left to go to the shop.

The girls were upset that Sanaa actually got locked up. They swore if they ran into Cocoa she was going to catch another beat down. They continued with their day taking appointments and walk in clients. Some of their walk in clients had to make appointments, because they still had to take Sanaa's appointments. The chaos was about to begin again at Spoiled Br@ Hair Technicians. They were used to it by now so it was routine for them.

Two O'clock came and Tamia was leaving the shop. She was on her way to Philly to Sanaa'a bail hearing. In no way was

Tamia trying to be late. She didn't want her baby seeing the inside of any prison walls.

"I hope this bail isn't ridiculous. Cocoa is definitely going to get hers if she is behind this. What part of the game is this? You start something with somebody and then call the cops when they finish it." Tamia thought to herself.

It was two thirty when Tamia walked inside the court room. She got there early so she could find out the bail and pay it. After all that Tamia and Sanaa been through they would've thought Tamia would be the one that needed a bail posted.

When Sanaa finally got her turn to see the judge she was relieved to see Tamia. The Judge set her bail at one hundred thousand dollars. Tamia almost fainted when she heard the amount. She only had to pay ten percent of it to keep Sanaa from going to a county prison. She still needed to give the court system ten thousand dollars and she only had five on her. Tamia immediately left for the bank to withdraw the other five thousand. In about a half hour she was back to post Sanaa's bail.

When Sanaa found out all of the charges that were being pressed against her she was devastated. She knew she whipped that girl but the charges weren't adding up. She was going to try to figure that out later but right then and there she wanted out of there.

"Thank you Mia I knew you weren't going to let me down." Sanaa said as she hugged Tamia the second she was released.

"You're welcome S you know I got my baby's back." Tamia responded.

"I don't know any other explanation but that incident with Cocoa. But the charges aren't adding up. You know I watch Court TV all day long so I know." Sanaa responded.

“Yeah I know you do. She is a fatal attraction case for real. This is ridiculous. How can someone be this crazy?” Tamia asked.

“I don’t know but I think you slept with that girl.” Sanaa responded.

“No I did NOT sleep with that girl I told you what happened. That was it no sexual contact except a kiss good night.” Tamia responded angrily.

“Well that was one hell of a kiss.” Sanaa responded sarcastically.

“Look I’m just as pissed off as you are. That bitch is taking this too far. Even if I broke up with you, what makes her think I would want her after this?” Tamia asked.

“I don’t know but you need to handle that. If you weren’t thinking about cheating or leaving me this wouldn’t have happened.” Sanaa responded.

“Yeah well if you weren’t acting like a nut. I wouldn’t have thought about it.” Tamia argued.

“Okay well look we aren’t going to get anywhere by arguing. So let’s focus on the situation at hand okay.” Sanaa responded rationally for the first time.

“Okay first you need a lawyer. So when we get to the shop grab the phone book and start looking. It’ll probably be too late because it’s almost five o’clock. So write down all of the ones you are interested in hiring and call them tomorrow.” Tamia responded.

“Well what about my clients?” Sanaa asked.

“We’ll take care of them while you look. Then you can do the ones that are left over.” Tamia answered.

“Okay Mia.” Sanaa responded.

They rode the rest of the way in silence. Tamia scrolled through songs and albums on her IPod. She finally found a song that she wanted to hear. “Can’t Hold me down” by Puff Daddy and Ma$e played while they drove to the shop. Tamia wanted something that would uplift Sanaa at the moment. She didn’t want her to lose it and get into more trouble.

When they made it to the shop Sanaa did exactly what Tamia told her to do. She spoke to the girls and her clients then went straight into the office and shut the door. Tamia explained to everyone why she wasn’t taking any clients at the moment. Sanaa’s clients were in shock to here that Sanaa was just arrested. They were dealing with her for years and she never struck them as that type of person.

After an hour and a half Sanaa joined the rest of the girls at the shop. Everyone had a million and one questions for Sanaa as soon as she did. Sanaa had developed a headache after ten minutes of question answering.

“Sanaa, how was it spending the day in a jail cell? I’ve never been locked up before.” Amber asked.

“And you don’t want to get locked up. The only thing I could do was, think of why I had a warrant and who could’ve pressed charges on me.” Sanaa replied.

“Well we think it was that bitch Cocoa. That’s the only person you had a fight with. That we know of anyway.” Keisha added to the conversation.

“I already came to that conclusion. Thank you. I had a lot of time to figure that shit out.” Sanaa responded with anger in her voice.

“Well did you find any lawyers that you might be interested in using?” Tamia asked.

"Oh yeah, I found ten of them. Five are in Media and five are in Philly." Sanaa replied.

"Okay good. Call the ones in Philly first they are more familiar with the system and judges in Philly." Tamia responded.

If Sanaa was on trial for one of the murders she committed then Tamia would let her pick her Lawyer on her own. But since she's about to do time for assault on Cocoa, Tamia was willing to help out in any way possible. She didn't want to see Sanaa go to jail for this psycho. The one thing that Tamia couldn't figure out was why Cocoa was going to great lengths to get to Sanaa. This couldn't be all about getting with Tamia. There had to be another reason behind it all. Tamia just couldn't put her finger on it but in the mean time she would remain silent about her thoughts.

"Okay Mia I figured you'd say that. That's why I wrote some down in Philly. I still can't believe I was locked up. My mom and Dad would have a fit if they found out." Sanaa said as she thought of her parents' reaction.

"I never met your parents but I could imagine. My parents would have one too if I was ever locked up." Amber replied.

The rest of the shop agreed with the statement. The more they sat around trying to figure out what all of the charges were, the more Sanaa got a headache. The last thing Sanaa wanted was to go to jail now. Sanaa was just about to get her happily ever after ending until this incident.

Sanaa's court dates kept getting postponed. In the meantime they had their grand opening for Spoiled Br@ Hair technicians 2. Tamia decided to run the shop in Philly since Sanaa was having legal trouble up there. Tamia took Amber with her and Keisha stayed with Sanaa. It wasn't before long that the clientele started pouring in at the new shop.

Amber was overwhelmed but that was what she wanted. She wanted clientele like Tamia and Sanaa. She wanted her own salon but didn't want to leave Tamia and Sanaa. She felt as though she needed to show them loyalty. But if the legal situation with Sanaa turned out ugly, she'd get a shot at becoming partner.

Spoiled Br@ Hair Technicians 2 was the talk of Philly within a month. They never saw anything like it. They heard of the one in Chester but didn't want to travel down there to get their hair done. It was the only shop that sold weave and other hair products. Everyone liked a one stop shop. Other salons started losing money before they knew it. That brought a lot of them to the shop to spy on Tamia and Amber. Tamia was willing to give them jobs if they were good stylist.

When Sanaa's trial was set to begin, Tamia had another Hair and Fashion Show planned. This one was going to put them over the top. The only thing was Sanaa was facing a jail sentence. Everything was going according to plan as far as the shop's expansion. The clothing line was also starting to take off. Tamia had her mind made up that she would start looking for a location to put her clothing store. It was time to put her styles on the market.

Sanaa's first day on trial was draining for her. She finally found out all of the charges when she hired a lawyer. She had an assault charge and a murder charge for a man she never even heard of. She was sure she would beat the murder charge. But when the trial went on for a few more days it didn't look good. Tamia and Sanaa started to worry. After two weeks on trial Sanaa was sentenced to fifteen to twenty years in prison. When the case was over she started punching her lawyer. Cocoa walked by her and said Ice was my brother bitch don't drop the soap. Sanaa immediately stopped hitting her lawyer and just sat down and stared at Tamia in a daze. Cocoa waited outside for Tamia as she watched them lock Sanaa up and take her away. When Tamia got outside the courtroom Cocoa approached her.

"Look I know you are wondering about my behavior but I am Ice's sister. I was in the apartment when she killed him. I saw the whole thing I had a key. When you three were in the bedroom I came in and I watched for a while. I was unarmed so I hid in the closet until you two left. I knew you were innocent so I left you out of it." Cocoa explained.

"I am so sorry about your brother. I didn't know. I thought you were more psychotic than she was. But she changed a lot even though I know you don't want to hear that." Tamia responded.

"Don't be I got my justice so I'm good now. But I can see what my brother saw in you. I recognized you as soon as I saw you in Tonyx If you would like to see me again I'm game. I still want to be with you. If not I understand, I'll see you later." Cocoa said before she walked to her car.

What goes around comes around. Be careful of what you put out there in the world because it can come back around. Sometimes in the same way as you dish out and sometimes in many different ways, but it always comes back. Karma is a Bitch. Stay positive and positive things will happen. When you find success, keep your head up and your nose at a friendly level.

The End

I have enclosed a bonus treat for you all who are becoming fans of my work. On the very next page is my next project Friend Zone which I hope all of you enjoy the sample of it. Give me some feedback on it. Send me a message on FaceBook or Myspace with any comments about it. Hope you enjoy.

Friend Zone

An Urban fiction
romance novel
written by

Tamika D. Harding

Chapter one:

The Bait

"Hi my name is Sensation but my friends Chocolate Ty, Candy, and Treasure all call me Sen. My nickname to everyone else is Goddamn because when I walk by a man the first thing he says is goddamn she's fine. I have a light brown complexion, long silky jet black hair, and a plump round booty that'll make a grown man cry. Last but not least I am five foot, seven inches tall and guaranteed to take you to heaven. If I were you ladies, I would put a short leash on my man. I've been known to turn them out and have them strung out on my love. My magnetic personality reels them in and once they're hooked my sex is like a drug they can't live without it. What more can I say about me? I'm the best that ever did it." Sensation spoke as she admired herself in the mirror.

Sensation would say this to herself as she looked in the mirror before showering every morning. She was gorgeous and no one could deny her of that. The one thing that people never knew about her was that she had very low self esteem. She would have sex with the ugliest guys she could find. Sensation also had all the talent in the world but lacked ambition to follow through with anything she had talent in. Many girls that knew of her often talked amongst themselves about her. Often times they would say that she was looking for a free ride but looks will only take her but so far.

Sensation never cared about what other people said about her. The only thing she knew is that she was twenty one and getting the money out of these guys she used as her play toys. She was spoiled by every guy she came in contact with regardless of the relationship.

Sensation even had a few female admirers. Some she chose when she wanted a little more excitement in the bedroom. The others she kept around for her companions. Needless to say she had both sexes eating out of the palm of her hand and she enjoyed every minute of it.

It was early one morning in the middle of the summer when sensation decided that she was going to call her lover up. Bear wasn't her boyfriend he was just her main play toy. But Bear was deeply in love with Sensation and would literally kill to be her man. The only time she wanted to be bothered with him was on her terms, which was when she wanted sex.

"Merry go round and around." Keith Sweat came through the speakers of Bear's phone.

"Hello." Bear answered.

"Hey, what are you doing later?" Sensation asked.

"I'll be hustling why what's up, do you want to go get something to eat or something?" Bear asked in an irritated tone.

"No I just want you to come fuck me in about an hour or two." Sensation replied.

"How come you can let me put my dick all up in you but I can't take you out, or stay the night, shit I can't even kiss you. What part of the game is that?" Bear asked out of frustration. He wanted Sensation to be his wife one day.

"Because I don't want anything else from you, just your dick, now come over here and fuck me like I said." Sensation demanded.

"Alright one day when I finally get fed up with this shit I'm going to tell you no." Bear responded before he hung up in her ear. He thought that would get to Sensation but it didn't she could care less.

After Sensation got off the phone she decided to take a long hot bubble bath before her play toy got there. She had Sade playing and five Aroma Therapy candles lit. As soon as she had everything in place Sensation slid her thick nicely shaped naked body into the bathtub.

She relaxed as she sang to Sade's "No Ordinary Love." Singing made her feel a lot more relaxed. After thinking about the sexcapade's her and Bear usually have she became aroused.

Sensation started touching herself as she soaked herself in the tub full of hot water and bubbles. A few minutes later she was masturbating, vigorously stroking her clitoris. She rubbed on her breast as she continued to stroke. She was ready to climax and didn't care if she woke up the neighbors. Sensation turned herself on with every moan she heard herself make. Before she knew it she exploded in the water.

"I needed that release. Now all I need is for Bear to come through and finish the job for me so I can send him on his way." Sensation thought to herself as she started to bathe.

"When he gets fed up he's going to tell me no. Yeah right no one can tell me no. No one can resist Sensation." Sensation continued to think to herself as she got out of the tub.

"I need a ride or die chick." The Lox came through the speakers of Sensation's phone.

"Hey." Sensation answered.

"Hey, what are you doing?" Treasure responded on the other end.

"I'm just getting out of the shower. I'm waiting for Bear to come over here." Sensation replied.

"Girl you need to stop playing with that boy. He already threatened you, telling you that you look like Lacy Peterson." Treasure responded in a concerned voice.

"Girl he's not going to do anything to me. He's just blowing smoke." Sensation responded nonchalantly.

"Yeah well you watch the First 48 so you know what people like him are capable of. I hate to see females like you who are in denial." Treasure tried to reason with her.

"I know he's capable of killing but I don't think he'll do anything to me." Sensation responded.

"Look I'm going to let you go so you can prepare for your Fuck session. If you're trying to chill with me then holler at me later." Treasure said before she hung up. Feeling like she was talking to a brick wall.

Treasure had only known Sensation for a year and a half but was undoubtedly in love with her. Treasure wasn't as experienced as Sensation when it came to dealing with females. But one thing for sure is Sensation had even Treasure turned out but she had more will power than Bear. Treasure never thought about a relationship with a female before Sensation. She had dealt with men all of her life. But Sensation was Bi sexual throughout her entire life. To Sensation playing with people's hearts was a game to her. She knew Treasure and Bear along with a number of others were in love with her but she continued to keep them around while stressing she didn't want a relationship.

"I want to break my lease so I can move. Cause you're a bug a boo, a bug a boo." Destiny's Child came through the speakers of Sensations phone.

"Hello Are you outside?" Sensation asked as she answered the phone.

"Yeah open the door." Bear responded angrily.

"Here I come now, don't try to be acting all like that. I'm not for the dumb stuff today okay, just fuck me and get out." Sensation snapped as she opened the door.

"I don't know what's up with you but if you want to get fucked then that's what you're going to get." Bear responded as he slammed the door.

"Don't be slamming my damn door and I told you my girlfriend got deported. I'm in love with her and only her I just use you to get me by sexually." Sensation responded as she took off the negligee she had on.

Bear wasted no time pushing her on the bed. He was already hard, just the sight of her did that to him. He unzipped his pants, put his condom on and rammed his manhood inside of her giving her hard, deep, and fast strokes every time he went in and out of her. He ejaculated after a half hour of that making sure she didn't get too much pleasure out of that. But unbeknown to him it was enough for her.

He wanted to stick around a while as usual so he lit up some marijuana knowing she couldn't resist smoking. That brought him another twenty minutes before he got put out. It was the same routine you'd think he'd get used to it or leave her alone but the boy was in love.

One day Sensation will fall in love with someone who will treat her the same way. She never saw it that way though. She was having her cake and eating it too.

Coming soon!!!!!

You can FaceBook me to give me your feedback on Friend Zone. All sales will go directly through me. These bookstores aren't playing fair so I'm boycotting them.

You can see me directly by calling (267) 584-6235, if you are in the Tri State area. Or order from my website: WWW.HustleWithFinesse.com or WWW.HustleWithFinesse.biz, you can also order from Amazon.com. Another option is send a check or money order payable to Tamika D. Harding

P.O. Box 81

Chester PA

19016

I hope to hear from you and remember tell a friend spread the word the bigger the audience the better. Thanks again for the love and support.

www.ingramcontent.com/pod-product-compliance
Lightning Source LLC
Chambersburg PA
CBHW070112260626
47160CB00004B/1437
* 9 7 8 0 6 1 5 3 5 2 3 8 1 *